PERILOUS KISS

THE BENEDICT BROTHERS
BOOK ONE

TARA SUE ME

Cover: 100Covers
Editing: Carol Taylor

ISBN:
Ebook 9781950017454
Print 9781950017461

PROLOGUE

Fifteen Years Ago
Secluded House
Outside Charleston, SC

"SIR! SIR!"

The man they called King stopped walking and took a deep breath. The damn nanny wanted to talk to him. Again. He'd spoken to her twice today already. What he really wanted to do at this point was to order her out of his house. Unfortunately, he couldn't afford such an action. She was the fourth nanny he'd hired in as many days and, according to the agency he'd been using, the last one they had available to send.

No matter what, this one had to work. He turned around to face her.

She quickened her step when she realized he waited, and in doing so was winded by the time she made it to where he stood.

1

According to her file, the young woman was twenty-three, but she didn't look a day over sixteen. Far too young for his taste. Not to mention, he preferred blondes and the woman/child before him was a brunette. Still, he had several clients who would be delighted with her. It was something to think about when the time came.

He plastered a frown on his face. "What is it?"

"I can't find her, sir."

Her voice trembled and that made him happy. People were always easier to handle if they feared you. Or feared what you would do to them. He kept his reply emotionless. "I assume you are referring to Jade, the five-year-old in your charge?"

"Yes, sir." The woman swallowed. Her entire body trembled. "She ran off when I turned around to get a book for us to read together. She's very smart for her age, sir..."

The nanny's voice trailed off at his upheld hand. "Enough," he said. "What is your name, again?"

"Constance, sir."

"Constance. What a horrible name." He shook his head. "However, your name is of little concern to me. What is my concern is your ability to do the job I hired you to do, and that job is to care for my ward. Would you agree?"

"Yes, sir."

He took a step closer and smelled her fear. Yes. Perfect. "I like to think of myself as a benevolent man, Constance. I took that little girl in after her mother's tragic death when no one else wanted her. That's benevolent, wouldn't you agree?"

"Yes, sir." She spoke in a hushed whisper.

"But as benevolent as I am, that benevolence has limits and your actions have surpassed mine." He paused to let that sink in before continuing, "I can't fire you. According to the agency, there's no one left to send. So all I can do is to ensure this doesn't happen again. Understood?"

"Yes, sir," she lied.

He laughed. "No, you don't. But you will."

Her eyes grew wide with fear and wider still when he snapped his fingers and two heavily muscled men appeared from the shadows, each taking one of her arms. "Nooo... nooo, sir."

"Take her to The Room and prepare her, but don't start until I arrive," he said.

"Sir?" Constance called, struggling unsuccessfully to get away from the brutes carrying her down the hall. "Sir!"

He waited until they had disappeared, and he could no longer hear her before turning to a large window. The floor to ceiling curtain covering it had moved slightly when he'd instructed his men to carry the nanny away. "Come out, Jade."

She appeared out from behind the curtain slowly. Small for her age, even for a girl, but the nanny had been correct about her intelligence. The young child would serve him well. Eventually.

As soon as she stepped away from the window, she stuck her left thumb in her mouth and sucked. A new and nasty habit, but one to be addressed at a later time. He had a bigger problem to deal with at the moment.

He bent down to her level when she stopped a few feet away from him. "Why did you run away from your nanny?"

She remained silent, sucking her thumb, staring at him with all-too-familiar eyes.

He tried again. "Jade. When I ask a question, I expect you to answer."

Her thumb fell out of her mouth with a pop and she gave him a sweet smile. She would probably be a great beauty one day. A smile like that would charm most people. Even he couldn't resist lifting the corner of his mouth in somewhat of a grin.

"Tell me why you ran away from your nanny," he tried again.

"I don't like you," she said before popping the same thumb back in her mouth.

Her words and actions were so unexpected and contradictory, he couldn't stop his laughter. Yes, taking the bastard child in was going to be a headache, but in the end, it would be worth the trouble.

CHAPTER I

"Damn," Keaton Benedict's oldest brother, Kipling, said. "You do know you're supposed to hit the red circle in the middle, right? Now I understand why you've never brought a woman home."

"Shut up, asshole." As the youngest of three boys, Keaton was used to his older siblings employing whatever means necessary to beat him at target practice. But Kipling had hit a new low with his last stunt.

"Not my problem you need help in finding the right spot." Kipling didn't even attempt to cover his amusement. "Do you need your older brother to give you some pointers?"

"No. What I need is for you to admit you timed your announcement to coincide perfectly with my shot." Keaton unloaded his gun and watched while Kipling lined up his own shot and hit the center of the target. Keaton shook his head. "You know I'm a better shot than you. The only way you ever win is by cheating."

Kipling grinned and started the process of unloading

and cleaning his own weapon. "Now that's where you're wrong. It wasn't cheating. It was strategy. Cheating would have been if what I'd told you was a lie."

Keaton had purposely focused on his brother's actions as opposed to his words because part of him hoped he had been lying. Unfortunately, not only had he lost to Kipling, but it appeared the news he'd shared while Keaton was taking his shot was true.

"Elise is really coming to stay with us this summer?" Keaton asked.

Kipling ran his hand through his dirty blond hair, just a touch lighter than Keaton's. All three of the Benedict brothers had the same coloring, right down to the light brown eyes that looked almost gold in the right light. Keaton remembered as a child how he wanted colored contacts because he got tired of people commenting on his eyes. It was only as he grew older that he'd learned to appreciate their uniqueness.

"Yes," Kipling said. "Her father asked if she could stay with us while she worked as an intern at a local law office."

Keaton bit his tongue so he wouldn't say what he wanted to. There was no way he could ever see Elise practicing law. Even with her family's move to New York years ago, she'd been groomed by her mother to be the perfect southern lady, and in her mother's eyes, the perfect southern lady did not work. Especially as a lawyer. Odds were the Germain family was simply using the internship as a way to get Elise to stay at Benedict House for the summer in the hopes Keaton would see her potential as a wife and be unable to keep himself from proposing.

There was a zero to none chance of that happening, but Mr. and Mrs. Howard Germain were old family friends, and

Howard had worked for his dad for years before retiring. Keaton wouldn't disrespect his brothers or his parents' memory by being anything other than polite to Elise.

He tried to push out of his mind memories of the summer before they went to college. They had only went out a handful of times, but that was all it'd taken to get a look at the real Elise.

"I don't understand why she couldn't find an internship closer to home," Keaton said. "Manhattan has more law firms than Charleston."

Kipling raised an eyebrow. "I didn't give the man the third degree. He asked if she could stay, and I said 'yes.'"

Keaton grunted in reply.

With their weapons unloaded and cleaned, they headed out of the country club's shooting range and walked toward the bar. It was tradition for the losing brother to buy drinks. They snagged a few stools and Kipling ordered for them both.

"I haven't said it, but I want you to know how glad I am to have you back home. I also wanted to discuss your future," Kipling said and looked up as the bartender brought their drinks over. "Thank you."

"I've told you repeatedly, I don't want anything to do with the family business." It was an argument they'd had numerous times over the past few years, and truth be told, Keaton didn't feel like getting into it again.

"I thought since you'd recently graduated, you might feel differently."

"You thought wrong," Keaton said. "Family business or not, I refuse to work for a company so diabolical."

Kipling lifted an eyebrow. "That's a bit over the top, wouldn't you say?"

"No, that's why I've been saying it for so many years."

"And yet, you have no qualms about enjoying the life-style or the private university education that diabolical business has provided you with."

Keaton bit his tongue to stop himself from replying because doing so would only make the situation worse. Besides, he knew it was hypocritical to refuse to work for the company that had financed his entire life.

At his side, Kipling let out a big sigh. "Look, I didn't mean for it to come out like that. I just..." He stopped and blew out a long breath of air.

Keaton took a sip of his scotch. He had the distinct impression Kipling was holding something back. Based on the way his older brother acted, that something was either big, unwelcome, or both.

It went without saying Kipling had a lot on his plate. As the oldest, he ran the family business, Benedict Industries. Though calling it a business again would likely result in his older brother kicking his ass. Empire, Kipling insisted, not business, and Keaton had already pressed his luck with the word enough times for one day.

The more he observed his older brother, the more certain he became that something else was going on. Though not apparent to the casual observer, the way Kipling sat seemed a bit off. Stiffer then normal, or maybe it would be more correct to say he was on high alert. But for what?

After sitting for a few more seconds in silence, Keaton finally asked, "Is there something you aren't telling me?"

Kipling opened his mouth, but before he could get a word out, a country club employee—from the administrative side and not the bar or restaurant based on the uniform—appeared at their side.

"Mr. Kipling Benedict?" the employee asked.

"Yes." Kipling frowned at the slender box the man held out.

"This was left at the reception desk for you."

Kipling eyed the box, but didn't take it. "By whom?"

The employee placed the box on the bar beside Kipling. "No one saw them. We have one staffer working the front desk, and she was talking with a member when this was dropped off." He raised an eyebrow. "Is there a problem, sir?"

Kipling sighed. "No. No problem. Thank you."

Keaton waited until the employee left. "What was that about?"

Kipling tapped the top of the box he'd not yet made a move to open. "It's nothing, I'm sure. More of a nuisance than anything."

"Have you received other ones that look like that?"

"Yes." Kipling slid the box closer and grasped the lid. "And if this one is like the others, it'll contain a single rose."

Keaton couldn't stop the gasp that left his throat when Kipling revealed the rose the box held. Not because his brother had been correct but because of flower's color. "Damn," he said when he got his voice back. "I didn't know roses came in black."

Kipling replaced the top back on the box. "Charming, isn't it? They've all been the same."

"How many have there been?"

"Half a dozen." Kipling waved the bartender over asked him to throw away the box. "They've always been delivered to the office before. This is the first one that didn't."

"I don't like it." If the roses weren't the reason for Kipling's odd behavior, Keaton couldn't help but think they weren't helping the situation.

"Me either, but it's pretty harmless, all things considered."

"Are you going to tell the police?" Keaton asked.

Kipling actually laughed. "Tell them what? That someone's sending me roses? Yes, I'm sure that would go over really well."

His brother could laugh it away all he wanted. There was something going on and Keaton was going to find out what it was.

TILLY BROCK DODGED the group of handsy businessmen as she dropped off a round of drinks at a nearby table. She hated this city. Hated everything about it. When she'd left eight years ago, her plan had been to never return. Yet here she was, the place where her childhood had gone from fairytale to horror story in less than a week's time. She'd done a relatively decent job of locking away the memories of that week and storing them in the far corners of her mind. Or at least she had until her mother's estate had finally been settled two months ago, nearly a year after her death.

Estate. A stupid word to use, in her opinion. Anything remotely resembling an estate had been sold or seized when her family was forced out of town. She would have laughed at the ridiculousness of it all if it wasn't for the fact that the word had destroyed the work of eight years and released all those locked away memories she swore to never revisit.

Two things led her to make the decision she once considered unfathomable. One, an old key her mother left.

Tilly assumed it opened a safety deposit box somewhere in Charleston. And the second and most puzzling, a request from Kipling Benedict for a face-to-face meeting.

She'd grown up with Kipling's younger brother, Keaton. They'd lived in the same neighborhood and gone to the same schools. Hell, at one point, she'd actually thought herself in love with him. Of course, that was *before*. Yet, even though she'd been close to Keaton all those years ago, she'd interacted with Kipling only a handful of times. Being so much older, he'd been away at college back when she spent every free minute with Keaton.

Though she'd not kept up with the Benedict family after leaving Charleston, there were a few things she did know about Kipling. One, he'd taken over the family business after his father's death, and two, you didn't say no when he requested a meeting.

That was the part hitting the hardest. The request didn't come from an assistant or some underling. It didn't come in the form of an email or phone call. It was a note he'd written by hand. Who did that anymore? More importantly, why did he want to meet with her? Why now, after all this time?

And the question she didn't want to admit having, but couldn't get out of her mind, what about Keaton?

Tilly had quit college when her mother became ill, and the money she'd planned to use for tuition had gone to help pay for medical bills and final expenses. She'd paid off the remaining debt by selling the small house she and her mother had lived in. With very little money and limited options, she ironically decided to try and start again in the very place she hated the most.

Which was why she was waiting tables at a low end

gentlemen's club. The *gentlemen* part was debatable, but the work was steady, tips were great, and the club had a strongly enforced no-touching-in-public-rooms rule.

On her way back to the bar, she sensed the weight of someone's stare. Not too surprising, she wasn't a dancer, but the outfit she was required to wear didn't leave much to the imagination.

Placing the tray on the bar, she rubbed the back of her neck as if in doing so she could rub out the feeling of being watched.

"Are you okay?" Raven, one of the bartenders asked.

Tilly genuinely liked Raven. She was friendly, cheerful, and spoke the truth in a way most people didn't. Plus, Tilly loved that she dyed her short hair a platinum blonde because she claimed to enjoy the way it clashed with her name.

"Just a feeling I'm being watched." Tilly laughed. "Which is stupid, right? How can I expect anything else when these shorts show off half my ass?"

Raven didn't reply. Instead, she scrubbed a spot on the bar top.

"Raven?" Tilly asked after several long silent seconds passed. She frowned. Tilly had only known her for a little over a month, but Raven had never been anything other than almost unbearably chipper.

"I think something's going on," Raven whispered without looking up. "I overheard two of the dancers say King was coming for a visit."

A shiver ran down Tilly's spine.

King not only owned the club and half the city, but ruled its deep dark corners as well. No one knew from where, though speculation ran from under city's streets to somewhere in Europe. No one had ever seen him. No one knew if King was his first or last name.

It was a given if you had anything to do with Charleston, he already knew who you were, but very few knew him. And those that did would never admit to it. Not if they wanted to live.

CHAPTER 2

W hat the fuck was he doing here? Keaton couldn't stop from asking himself for what had to be the six-hundredth time.

"There we go. Finally," an old high school friend, Michael said as the lights around them dimmed and everyone's attention turned to the stage at the front of the club. "Time for dancing."

Keaton wished he'd turned Michael down when he called not long after Keaton and Kipling had returned home from the country club the day before. If not that, he should have suggested a better place than this joint. Instead, he'd agreed to met his longtime friend, and once upon a time's troublemaking cohort, for a night of debauchery.

Two scantily clad women strutted out onto the stage, but Keaton was too far away to see details. All he could make out were tiny bikinis tops and even tinier thongs. Blondes. Both of them dancing with moves choreographed enough to make any red-blooded man fantasize about ripping off the scraps of fabric and fucking her on the stage right in front of everyone.

What did it say about him that the idea held little appeal?

A movement to the side of the stage caught his eye. A server. Female. He only saw her profile, but there was something about her. What was it?

He slid off the barstool to get a closer look.

"Hey, man," Michael called after him. "Where are you going?"

Keaton didn't reply.

"Benedict?" Michael tried again.

Keaton shook his head. He wasn't a stranger to the numerous clubs around the city catering to wealthy men and their carnal needs. However, he'd never been the type to single out any particular woman while at one. After all, he'd always said, one half-naked woman was just as good as another. A point made evident by the number of times his picture was in the society pages, though never with the same woman twice.

And yet, here he was, eyes fixed on the petite waitress off to the side of the stage, trying to blend into the background and not take away from the dancing duo. She was failing horribly. He wasn't sure why the management felt the need to put anyone on stage with her working here. Did they actually expect people to look at those two with *her* in the room?

She moved with a grace that made the two blondes look like ducks swimming alongside a swan. She stretched out her hand to pass a glass to a man sitting on the far inside of a booth. Everyone in the vicinity turned to watch her lithe body. Keaton included.

It sounded so crazy, he couldn't even verbalize it, but he thought he knew her from somewhere. Something about the way she moved called to him and urged him forward for a better look.

He took a step in her direction.

She was magnificent and continued to captivate the audience near her. Keaton's eyes traveled over her body, taking in as many details as possible: her light brown skin, the curve of her hips, and the slope of her breasts covered by a tight cropped shirt. Her skin would be oh-so-soft to touch. His eyes drifted higher at the same time she turned her head his way and he froze.

Tilly.

He couldn't breathe. It couldn't be.

What was she doing in Charleston? The last he'd heard, her family had moved to Texas. Granted, they'd both been fourteen at the time, but he'd never forgotten the day he'd arrived home from school, walked into the eerily quiet kitchen, and discovered his life had changed forever.

Before that day, Tilly had always stopped at his house after school to help him with his homework. Usually her mother would come over and gossip with his mom. But there was nothing that day. He'd looked out the back door to get a peek of their house and gasped. All over the yard were men carrying furniture.

He'd sped back inside and up the stairs to his mother's room and, with a stomach filled with dread, asked where Tilly and her mom were.

His mother arched a perfectly shaped eyebrow. "They're moving to Texas," she said, and his world shifted out of focus.

"Why?" he managed to croak out. Texas was so far away. It made no sense why they would move away from their family.

"Mr. Brock has been embezzling money from your father."

"What?" It wasn't possible. Not Tilly's dad. He was stealing from them? Something didn't sound right.

His mother gave him a sad smile. "I'm afraid he was caught red-handed. The Brock family is basically ruined now. The best thing for them to do is to start over somewhere else."

His parents had always joked about him and Tilly getting married one day. Everyone talked about it, and he didn't care because Tilly was smart and pretty. The week before, he'd kissed her for the first time. Her lips had been soft and sweet and he'd looked forward to kissing them over and over. How could he kiss her if she was in Texas?

"Your father's going to promote Howard Germain. Isn't his daughter in your class, too?"

Elise. Tilly's best friend. Or was her best friend. He felt sick. He mumbled a half intelligible answer to his mom and ran down the stairs to the living room. He had to call Tilly. Had to talk to her, even if it was only to say goodbye.

But their phone had already been disconnected, and when he went to their house, the men moving all the furniture told him they'd already left.

TILLY TOOK a deep breath and muttered, "Excuse me, please," to the man blocking the path to her customer. She recognized the move for what it was, an attempt to make her reach across him. She grit her teeth and made sure the men saw just enough cleavage as she handed the drink to the waiting customer.

"Thank you, darling." He spoke directly to her chest,

never once looking her in the eyes. "Why ain't someone as pretty as you up on stage?"

Like she didn't hear *that* ten times a night. Her mother might not roll over in her grave at the thought of her daughter serving drinks at a gentlemen's club, but Tilly knew she'd come back from the dead for the sole purpose of slapping her upside the head if she even thought about dancing topless.

"Two left feet," she told the guy.

"Trust me." His laugh gave her chills. "It ain't your feet we're interested in."

She bit her tongue to keep from replying.

On stage, the dance currently being performed by a set of twins was coming to an end. One of the blonde twins glared at her, and in doing so, tripped and almost fell. Several men booed. The other twin shot Tilly a look. Like it was Tilly's fault her sister was so clumsy. Oh well, what else was new? It wasn't a day ending in 'y' if she didn't piss off the Wonder Twins.

Tilly gathered several empty glasses and nodded as a few drink orders were given. Her tray was heavy, but it was nothing she couldn't handle. She turned to head in its direction when she once again felt someone's eyes drilling holes into her from the back of the room but more intensely this time. She lifted her head to find out who.

A quick scan showed no one out of place. She looked again and saw him, standing slightly off to the side, watching her with an easy confidence. Her body hummed because the tilt of his head somehow seemed familiar. He recognized her the same instant she recognized him.

Keaton Benedict.

Her tray fell to the floor.

CHAPTER 3

Tilly blinked, and he was gone. Just that quickly, he'd disappeared. Had it really been him or had she imagined him?

"Damn, klutz."

"I think I stepped on some glass."

"These are two hundred dollar shoes."

Unfortunately, she did not imagine the mess she'd made, the angry customers, or Mr. Granger, the manager, standing near the bar with his arms crossed. The twins, wearing matching see-through wraps, stood beside him, both with evil grins.

Shit.

Not only had she made a godawful mess, but Tilly knew the twins would spin things to make her out to be the only one at fault. Granger, of course, would believe them. According to the rumors floating around the club's staff, he was sleeping with both twins.

Tilly held up her hand before he could talk. "I take full responsibility. It won't happen again."

"Clean it up and then come to my office." He slapped one twin on the ass. "Good job as always, girls."

She bent down and started picking up the larger pieces of glass. Not for the first time, she missed Janie, who used to work the bar, but had moved to Washington, DC with her fiancé. If Janie had still been working, not only would she have come over to help, but she'd crack a joke or two and make Tilly laugh as well.

"Need some help?" a voice from her past asked.

Her hand slipped and the sharp edge of a glass shard sliced her skin. "Damn it." She shook her finger, trying not to let the threatening tears escape. Damn it all to hell. She hated this place. This city. This state.

In a swift move, Keaton knelt beside her, took the tray from her other hand, and started picking up fragments of glass.

"I feel as if I need to apologize." He never stopped what he was doing and didn't look at her. "I don't believe you would have dropped anything if it had't been for me."

She opened her mouth but nothing came out. What did you say to someone you'd spoke with every day for eight years and then didn't see for another eight? Not that it mattered, seeing as how she'd momentarily lost the ability to speak.

Instead, she sat on her heels while doing her best not to flash the entire club with her underwear. She took a deep breath and tried again.

"No, it's not your fault." She took a few seconds to study him. He hadn't changed all that much. He'd always been ridiculously handsome and had matured into a devilishly handsome man. The lanky frame of the teen she knew had been replaced by solid muscle. His hair was the same dirty blond, though, and his eyes were the same light brown that looked almost golden in the right light. All three of the Benedict brothers had that odd eye color.

Out of the corner of her eye she saw Granger watching her. He wouldn't like the fact that a customer was helping. She reached for a large chunk of glass the same time Keaton did and their hands brushed. She jerked away.

He held her gaze. "Tilly..."

He hesitated and before he could finish, a silver stiletto stepped between them. "Hello, handsome," Twin One said. "Why don't you come with me?"

"Are you here to help?" Tilly asked, when what she wanted to ask was *Just what the hell do you think you're doing?*

"You have got to be kidding," she said, shaking her head and making her blonde waves bounce around her shoulders. "Mr. Granger sent me."

"Why?" Keaton asked in a hard voice Tilly didn't recognize. She glanced at him, surprised at how angry he looked.

Twin One shrugged, seemingly indifferent to his tone. "He thought you needed more than she could provide," she said with a pointed look at Tilly. "You're to come with me for a private dance."

Tilly was used to the barely concealed barbs, but seriously? She acted like she wasn't listening to the conversation, afraid if she didn't, she'd blurt out something that would get her in more trouble than she was already in.

Keaton picked up the last big shard of glass and put it on the tray. "I think it's clear to anyone looking that I'm busy helping an employee. I'd also like to point out that no one else is."

Before Tilly could say it was fine and she didn't need help, Twin One replied, "It's okay. Really. She gets paid to do that."

"And I know exactly what you get paid for." Keaton was still watching the blonde as he took his wallet out of his pocket and peeled off several bills. Tilly couldn't see the amount from where she stood, but the other woman's eyes grew large. "I assume this will cover the cost of a dance?"

Tilly eyed him in disgust while trying to avoid what she knew would be a seething look of victory from the blonde. As it was, she couldn't miss the sultry, "Oh yes, this will give you the full package," given in reply.

Desperate to get away, Tilly turned to take her tray back to the bar, but Keaton put a hand on her arm, forcing her to stop.

"Good," Keaton said. "Then take it to your manager and tell him the dance isn't wanted or needed."

"What?" the blonde asked, and Tilly couldn't help but smile. "We can't take your money and not give you anything in return."

Tilly watched in satisfaction as the twin handed the money back to Keaton. With a toss of her head, she walked toward the employees lounge.

Keaton waited for her to disappear from sight before speaking. "I'm sorry we got interrupted, but I don't think this is the best time to chat. When do you get off?" He hesitated. "That is, if you want to chat with me."

She should have expected to run into Keaton at some point and made a plan on how to deal with it. Seriously, she had finally pushed herself to make an appointment to meet with his brother. Why hadn't she considered she might run into Keaton. "I don't think I have anything to say to you."

Disappointment or regret, surely it couldn't have been guilt, flashed in eyes. "Tilly."

"I haven't been living under an assumed name, if you

had wanted to chat sometime over the last eight years, you could have looked me up. Your brother did."

Keaton's jaw dropped, and she took the opportunity to carry the tray back to the bar.

"Want to talk about it?" Raven asked.

Tilly shook her head. "Granger wants to see me."

Seconds later, she stepped out from behind the bar on her way to his office. *Pull yourself together.* She closed her eyes, attempting to calm herself and tripped. Fortunately, she found her balance before faceplanting on the floor.

Looking around, she saw the second twin watching her with glee. "You can't even walk; no wonder you get bar duty."

Anger surged through her, but Tilly spoke soft enough so only the twin would hear her. "I'd rather have bar duty than have to suck old man dick. How long did it take Granger to come? Sore mouth?"

"You bitch!" The twin took a swing, and Tilly lifted her arms to shield her face. Instead, she inadvertently upended the tray of a nearby server, and for the second time that night, Tilly stood in a mess of glass and booze.

A security guard wandered over to see what was happening. Not surprising since they'd once more captured the attention of the entire crowd.

The guard stood over the mess on the floor. "What's going on here?"

"Don't look at me," the twin said, pointing at Tilly. "She's the one who did it. I told her she didn't have the talent to be a dancer, and she got all mad and started swinging."

"You lying..." Tilly told herself to remain calm. She looked up to the guard. "You know she's lying, right? I mean you were standing right there. You saw everything."

"I didn't see nothing," he said, and Twin Two's eyes flashed in victory.

"Ohhh, I think I have glass in my foot. Help me?" the blonde asked, holding out her hand and fluttering her eyelashes.

Tilly sighed. She should have known better than to deliberately piss off either of the twins. It never ended well for her, and since the twins literally held the manger's balls, it never would.

JADE

I don't have many memories from my childhood. Most of my life before the age of six or seven is made up of hazy images or whispered words having as much probability of being memories as they do of being dreams. But there is one scene I'm almost positive I remember.

I was five. That's the reason I think it actually happened, because my age is such a certainty. I was five and had experienced a horrible nightmare about my mother. I remember waking up and screaming. Seconds later, a woman who was not my mother came into my room and pulled me into her arms.

As I cried and told her about the nightmare, she rocked me in her arms and told me all was well. She assured me my mother was in heaven and watching over me. Her voice sounded so soothing and her embrace so warm, I had no problem believing her. To this day, I often look to the sky and wonder if my mother still watches.

Sometimes I hope she doesn't.

My first know-for-sure memory is the day I turned seven. King had told me it was a special day because he was going to let me in on his big secret. I'd barely been able to keep still that morning while I waited for him to come and get me.

King wasn't my father, but I had a feeling he knew who was. Especially since he always told me about how worthless my mother was and that I was the only good thing she'd left behind. For some reason, I assumed his big secret concerned my father. That I would at least learn his name.

When it was finally time, I all but bounced down the hall at King's side and my heart started to race as he unlocked his office door and motioned for me to follow inside. It was a room I'd previously been forbidden to enter and I felt like a princess walking beside King into his private lair.

Six men sat around a large round table that nearly filled one side of the room. I thought it looked how I'd always pictured Camelot, except King would be Arthur with the men as his knights. All six watched me with unveiled interest. Was one of them my father?

I looked from face to face, trying to guess who it could be.

"Gentlemen," King said. "Let me introduce you to the one who will aid us in destroying the Benedict family."

The men smiled at me, and though I wasn't sure what King meant, an uneasy feeling crept into my body. How would it be possible for me, at age seven, to destroy anyone? I couldn't make sense about anything King had said, and my stomach dropped as I realized I wouldn't be learning about my father.

How could I have been so wrong about what King had planned? It wasn't until that moment it hit me how badly I wanted to know something about my parents other than what a disappointment my mother had been.

I parted my lips to speak. It was on the tip of my tongue to tell King how rotten his surprise was when I felt his hands on my shoulders, squeezing. Hard. It was as if he knew I was getting *ready to say something even though I knew that to be impossible because he stood behind me.*

"You're going to make me proud, aren't you?" King's grip didn't lessen a bit as he asked the question, the pain from his hands bringing tears to my eyes.

I blinked them away, not wanting anyone to see me cry. "Yes, Sir."

That memory from my seventh birthday was forefront in my mind as I stood before King in the same office thirteen years later. The round table still filled half of the space, but it was empty today. King sat behind his desk, studying me. He didn't look pleased.

He sighed heavily, and I was so focused on trying to figure out what was wrong with him and recalling my actions over the past week to make sure I hadn't done anything deserving of his displeasure, I almost missed the subtle shift of the air off to my left side.

Almost.

In less than three seconds, I had one of King's men, Kevan, restrained with his hands behind his back and my knife at his throat. I looked at King expectantly. I'd practiced my expressions religiously over the past few years and rarely did anyone see anything other than what I wanted them to see.

At the moment, I hoped my expression masked how much I didn't want to kill Kevan. He was my age, and while I wouldn't call him a friend, we'd always had a mutual sort of respect for each other. I didn't want to kill Kevan, hell, I had a bit of a crush on him, however, if King ordered me to, I wouldn't have a choice.

King waved his hand. "Let him go."

I dropped Kevan immediately. He scrambled to his feet and stood in silence waiting for instruction from King.

"You disappoint me, Kevan," King said. "I expected a much better showing."

Kevan wisely didn't comment. Instead, he lowered his gaze to the floor. My heart pounded because I knew the kill order could still come. The seconds seemed to drag until King spoke again.

"Leave us," he told Kevan. "And practice."

Kevan bowed. "Yes, sir."

King waited for him to leave the office before addressing me. "You did well."

His voice rarely held emotion, but praise from him was even rarer, and I took my wins whenever possible. I struggled not to show how happy those few words made me.

"Thank you, sir." My voice, thankfully, sounded neutral.

"It's time." He sighed and stood. "I trust you're prepared for what that entails."

It wasn't posed as a question, but I answered anyway. "Yes, sir."

There was one thing and one thing only that had been poured into my head since that long ago birthday. The Benedict family was evil, and it was up to me to put an end to them. I'd asked King once, not long after that day, what they'd done. His eyes had glowed with a burning rage I'd never seen before and have never seen since. In a tight and low voice, he said they'd killed someone who was very dear to him and had almost ruined him financially. I'd nodded and he added that if I was smart, I'd never bring it up again. His tone was so murderous, I vowed never to do so.

"I'm not sure you are ready." His flat gray eyes pierced me. "But it hardly matters. We have to move now, and whether you're ready or not, you will do this and you will not fail."

When I was a child, I thought King only had to speak and

the universe would do his bidding. To be honest, part of me still believed that to be the case.

"Never, sir. I will never fail you."

He walked to the minibar off to the side of the room and poured two drinks.

I picked up the glass he placed in front of me. "Here's to the end of the Benedict Empire."

He lifted his glass and joined in my toast. "Here's to breaking it beneath our feet, lighting it on fire, and making them watch it burn."

CHAPTER 4

Keaton seethed as he drove home, questions swarming inside his head. Which one of his brothers had reached out to Tilly? What had they contacted her about? Why was tonight the first he'd heard about it?

It had to have been Kipling, if only because his oldest brother had been at college all those years ago.

It wasn't until he pulled into the drive at Benedict House he realized he'd never told Michael he was leaving. He shot off a quick text once he parked, telling him something had come up at home he had to deal with.

Knox's car wasn't in the garage, so it appeared Kipling was the only one inside at the moment. Probably for the best, he decided. One-on-one was always better than for him to go after both of his brothers at once.

He schooled his expression in case he ran into their housekeeper, Maggie, who had worked for them since he was in diapers. Fortunately, the path to the downstairs office he felt certain Kipling was still working in was clear.

His older brother did a double take at his entry and

stood behind the massive desk that had once belonged to their father. "Keaton? What's wrong?"

"Why the hell didn't you tell me you'd been in contact with Tilly Brock?"

Kipling's expression dissolved into an *oh-so-that's-what-this-is-about* look that Keaton wanted to wipe off his face with his fist.

Kipling waved at the chair at Keaton's side. "Sit down."

Keaton didn't want to sit, but Kipling wouldn't say another word until he did, so he stifled his sigh and took a seat.

"Thank you," Kipling said. "Now, to answer your question, I didn't see a need to tell you. It's a personal, business decision and you've been very clear with your opinion about anything pertaining to business."

"What the fuck kind of business decision involving Tilly is personal?"

Kipling raised an eyebrow. "Decided you want be part of the evil conglomeration that is Benedict Industries, after all, have you?"

His brother's nonchalant attitude did nothing to calm him. "Don't make me kick your ass."

Kipling leaned back in his chair, coolly regarding Keaton as if he hadn't just threatened him."You and Tilly were close back then, weren't you?"

"Yes," Keaton replied.

"It wasn't done on purpose. I didn't realize how much she meant to you."

Keaton could only nod. His brothers might annoy the shit out of him, but they'd never do anything to hurt him intentionally.

"I have a meeting with Tilly the day after tomorrow at

the harbor-side office. I'd requested to meet with her several months ago, but she's only recently accepted."

"How long have you been in contact with her?"

Kipling gave him a long stare before replying. "I typically only dealt with Anne, but when she died and her estate was settled, issues came up and I need to speak to Tilly. That's why she's coming."

Keaton's body went numb with his brother's words. "Anne died?"

His mind tried to piece together what he'd just heard. Tilly's mom had died? Anne had been so full of life, so carefree and joyous. The type of person everyone wanted to be around, that was Anne. His heart clenched as the ramifications hit him.

Tilly.

He'd heard her father had passed away following a heart attack and now she'd lost her mother. They had been such a close and loving family, but Tilly was their only child. And now she was alone.

"How?" he finally managed to ask.

"Breast cancer."

Keaton blinked away the tears that threatened to fall. "You should have told me."

"I see that now. I'm sorry."

Without a word, Keaton nodded and got up to leave. It was the first time in his entire life he'd ever heard his brother apologize.

KEATON JERKED WIDE AWAKE the next morning at the sound of someone walking down the hall. It took a few seconds for him to realize it was Knox. Surprised, he rolled over to look at the time. Five-thirty. That didn't sound like Knox. He'd never known the middle Benedict brother to get less than eight hours of sleep a night.

Knowing he wouldn't be able to go back to sleep, he decided to go ahead and get up. The one good thing about the early hour was he could go for a jog before the heat and humidity of the day settled in so thick and heavy it felt like he was breathing water.

He yawned, forcing himself to get moving. He'd tossed and turned most of the night thinking about Tilly, Anne, and everything that went down years ago. He'd never completely bought the story that Mr. Brock had embezzled money from the company. Not Mr. Brock with his easy-going nature and strong sense of compassion, whose kindness was surpassed only by his wife. And quite possibly, his daughter.

On his way out the door, he passed Maggie and turned down her offered coffee. She relented only after getting him to promise he'd be back in time for breakfast. Once outside, he took a deep breath and started with a slow and steady pace, warming up his muscles before settling into the brisk pace he enjoyed.

Though there were a few people already out and about, Keaton found himself alone with his thoughts for the most part. Not wanting to rehash his interaction with Tilly for the millionth time, he quite purposely focused on his conversation with Kipling about becoming part of the family business.

He loved this city and his family. But he understood how it might not appear that way based on his words. He loved Charleston's charm and strength. The diversity of the people. The taste of its cuisine. Yes, he was proud of his heritage and the role his family had played.

As he ran, he looked out toward the water at his side.

The water that was life to his family's shipping empire. He could hear Kipling asking if he was so proud of what his family had accomplished, why did he reject being part of the company they'd created?

That question had bothered Keaton until he went on his first international relief trip the summer before his sophomore year in college. Then he knew the answer immediately. To him, it wasn't enough to simply make the most money and wield the most power. To be fulfilled, he needed more. For as much as he loved his city, he wasn't blind to her problems.

Charleston had a history that couldn't be washed away or overlooked. There were inequalities and perceptions that had to be acknowledged and dealt with. Poverty and abuse still filled the cobbled streets. And as much as he'd enjoyed his work overseas, he couldn't see tackling someone else's home before straightening out his own.

That was what he wanted to do with Benedict Industries. It wasn't enough that they were shipping giants. He wanted them to be giants of charity, too. But it went beyond charity. There had to be a way to not only help the people of Charleston but to set them on an upward path.

Sometimes, it felt like a burden too heavy to carry alone.

He should ask Knox. He was the heart of the three brothers. The true good-doer. If he wasn't able to help, Keaton was willing to bet he knew someone who would. It would be better to discuss his ideas with Knox before he even thought about bringing them up to Kipling.

He turned and started back toward the house. Maybe Knox would be at breakfast and he'd be able to set up a time to talk with him then.

More people were out and about on his way back home. He slowed his pace as he approached the house. A glance at his watch showed he had time to shower before making his way to the dining room for the breakfast he'd promised Maggie he'd have.

He couldn't help but smile when he thought of the petite woman he considered part of the Benedict family. Her hair was now more gray than the vivid red he remembered from his childhood, and he was fairly certain it wasn't his imagination that she was shorter. None of that mattered, however. He'd told her to expect him for breakfast and nothing short of death or a natural disaster would keep him from the table.

By THE TIME Keaton made it home and showered, Knox had already left for the harbor-side offices. Since he'd promised Maggie he'd eat breakfast, he made a quick call to Knox and set up a time to meet later in the morning for a late coffee break.

"Come on in, Keaton," Knox said a few hours later. "Just let me grab my jacket and we'll go chat."

Keaton gave a friendly, "hello" and, "how are you" to the two admins that ran their front office and kept everything organized. Both ladies looked up at him and smiled.

"Can I bring either one of you something back to eat?" Knox asked straightening his tie after reappearing with his jacket on. "Barbara? Joy? I heard they had chocolate croissants today."

Barbara was in her late fifties and had been working for Benedict Industries for as long as Keaton could remember. "Nothing for me." She waved them away.

Joy was only few years younger. "You know if I even look at bakery food I gain ten pounds."

"I know nothing of the kind," Knox said with a smile.

"Do you have to flirt with every female over the age of twenty-one?" Keaton asked once they were on their way.

"That wasn't flirting. That was me being nice. Want to see me flirt? I can flirt."

Keaton didn't doubt it. Hell, half the things Knox did would come across slimy and creepy if any other man tried to do them. But for some reason, women swooned at Knox.

As they walked to their favorite coffee spot, Keaton counted no less than five women who said hello to Knox in passing. Keaton shook his head. All that attention and to Knox it was no big deal.

Which struck him as odd. Knox had never been one to turn down any type of female attention, and he'd always made it a point to bring up the name of whichever socialite he was with at the moment. How long had been since he last remembered Knox talking about his current fling? Weeks? Months?

"Damn." Keaton stopped. "I can't believe I didn't see it before."

"See what?" Knox asked, pulling him out of the middle of the sidewalk.

"Who is she and why haven't you introduced her to the family?"

Keaton didn't know it was possible to look that deathly pale and not pass out. For all that he might try to deny it, Keaton knew he'd guessed right.

Knox had a girlfriend.

A secret one.

Keaton smiled and started walking again. "That's okay. You don't have to tell me. Obviously, you're keeping it a secret for some reason."

Nope. He didn't have to know who she was or why they didn't tell anyone about their relationship. Not yet, anyway.

For now, it was enough to know she existed. He was glad his playboy older brother had found someone.

Knox didn't say anything, but soon caught up to him. Keaton refrained from glancing his way, and it wasn't until they made it to the restaurant that Knox spoke.

"It's not for the reason you think," he said. "It's ...well... we're complicated."

Knox looked troubled. Because he didn't like keeping his relationship hidden or because Keaton had figured it out?

"I don't *think* anything," Keaton said. "It's not my business. Just don't go getting married without telling me, okay?"

This time, Knox turned positively green. Keaton punched his older brother on the shoulder. "You need to loosen up some. Seriously, you'll tell us when you're ready."

Knox nodded and looked slightly better. By the time they ordered and found a corner table, he appeared to be back to his normal self.

"What did you want to talk with me about?" Knox asked when they were settled with their drinks.

"It's an idea I had for Benedict Industries," Keaton replied.

"You have an idea for the business?" Knox leaned back in his seat. "That'll make Kip happy."

"Yeah, he's been on my ass about working for the company."

"He means well. Just doesn't always come across that way." Knox sipped his coffee. "But tell me about this idea you have."

"It struck me during my summers overseas."

"The ones in India with the water project?"

Knox would know about his not-so-public summers

just as Keaton knew about his middle sibling's own summers overseas. Except Knox spent his time learning about computer hacking. "Yes. It occurred to me that I'm in a position, well, *we* are in a position, to give back. To do so in a way few people are because of how successful the business has been."

While he talked, Knox listened intently, nodding at what he said.

Keaton continued. "I'd like to create a division within Benedict Industries to give back tangibly to our community. It's not only in India that people need help. It's right here in our backyard."

"Damn," Knox said.

"What?"

"I'm just mad I'm not the one who came up with it." Knox waved toward him. "Creating a charitable division of Benedict Industries."

"Do you think Kip will go for it?"

"It'll create a lot of good PR. He'll care about that, and he'd like to help people, too. Do you plan to do this all on your own?"

"Probably. At least to start. I wanted to put a proposal together for Kip. Will you look at it before I give it to him?"

Knox nodded. "I think it's a great idea and you definitely have my support. After you write the proposal, we'll approach Kip together."

It was the outcome Keaton had hoped for and he felt as if a huge burden had been lifted off him. He could work for the family business and do something he felt passionate about.

CHAPTER 5

Two days after seeing Keaton at the club, Tilly wasn't surprised to find him with Kipling when she arrived for their meeting. She did her best to focus on Kipling and not to look at or think about Keaton, despite the way her body nearly hummed at his nearness.

Kipling greeted her warmly and said how sorry he'd been to hear about her mother's passing. He nodded toward Keaton. "I didn't invite him."

Tilly cringed, but didn't say anything. Obviously, she sucked at coming across indifferent.

"I told him he could only stay with your approval," Kipling added.

Tilly risked turning toward the man standing at her side. In the days following her family's move from Charleston, she remembered thinking it would only be a matter of time before the Benedicts realized how wrong they were. Even if they didn't, she knew Keaton would contact her somehow. It was unfathomable to think he believed her father stole from them.

But as days became weeks that grew into months, it

became clear he'd done just that. Her heart still ached to recall how much it hurt the day she accepted she'd never again see the boy she'd seen every day for eight years. And though she tried to convince herself that the boy she'd shared everything with from secrets to first kisses was no more, a part of her refused to believe it.

She studied the man he was now and wondered if there was any trace of the boy she once knew inside. It wasn't clear, but she held out the slim chance there was. Or at least, that's how she justified her response.

"He can stay."

Keaton let out a sigh of relief.

Kipling nodded. "Very well, let's have a seat."

Tilly sat, still acutely aware of the man at her elbow and hoped she hadn't made a mistake by letting him stay.

"I'm sure you've been wondering why I asked you to meet with me," Kipling said. "About nine months ago, we received a letter inquiring about a life insurance policy for your mother that had been taken out around ten years ago. The letter was from an attorney in Miami, which by itself isn't odd, but what puzzled me was that I couldn't find any of the records mentioned in his letter.

"The more I looked into the matter, the more files I found missing. Numerous business records, including financials and invoices. All of which was troubling enough, but large sections of the databased backup files are also gone, including calendars and emails."

He paused for a second, and Tilly couldn't stop from thinking the worst.

"And that's why you wanted to meet with me?" she asked, forcing herself not to give into the rage surging through her veins. "You think my dad took them and I now have all that information?"

"No," Kipling said, his calm tone the complete opposite of her own. "I asked you to meet with me because I found the policy. But since you brought it up, I believe Dad was wrong about your father. I was away at college when it all went down, but I remember thinking how strange it all seemed. Discovering how many records are missing from that period of time only seems to confirm my suspicion."

"Nothing about it ever made sense to me, either," Keaton said. "I've never believed Mr. Brock capable of stealing from anyone, and Dad was his friend. Remember how they played golf every Saturday?"

"And Anne and Mom were always doing something for that garden club they loved so much." Kipling tapped his fingers on his desk. "With those papers missing, though, it's all just speculation, and I can't prove anything."

"But you found the insurance information?" Keaton asked.

Stunned at the revelation that both brothers thought her father was innocent, Tilly found herself unable to speak until Kipling picked up a few papers from his desk and passed them to her.

"What's this?" She glanced at the one on top.

"The life insurance policy," Kipling said.

A hefty one, too.

More than enough for her to move back to Texas if she wanted, finish school, and possibly have a little left over as a nest egg.

She shook her head and handed the papers back. "I can't take this."

"Yes, you can," Keaton started and probably would have kept talking except Kipling lifted his hand and motioned for him to be quiet.

"Legally, it's your money," Kipling said. "Your father paid for the policy, no questions asked."

"I can't," she repeated, though part of her wanted nothing more than to grab the papers and run as far away as possible. "With the history between our families...no, I can't."

"What the hell are you talking about?" Keaton all but yelled. "Yes, you can. If nothing else it'll get you out of that hell hole you work at."

"Which thanks to you, I can't go to for the next week," she shot back and immediately regretted.

"What do you mean?" Keaton asked.

"Nothing." She hadn't wanted him to know. "Really, it's not."

"I don't believe you." Years ago, he could always tell when she lied. It appeared he still did.

"It's fine, I promise." She stood. The room felt too hot. She had to get outside and catch her breath. Try to make sense out of everything she'd just heard. "Speaking of, I need to go and pick up my check."

Mr. Granger sent her a text the day before telling her stop by before they opened to pick it up. She thanked both brothers and headed for the door, not stopping or slowing even though she heard footsteps behind her.

"Tilly! Wait!" Keaton called as she made it outside. "Where's your car?"

She'd sold it as soon as she'd arrived in Charleston to pay for a place to stay, but she wasn't going to tell him that. "I'm walking."

"It's over four miles."

Yes, it was, and that would give her plenty of time to think. She kept walking.

"Tilly, please." Keaton sounded borderline desperate. "At least let me drive you."

She relented and agreed to let him drive. She tried to tell herself it was because the sky looked like rain, but she knew better. Deep inside, a part of her she'd never admit to having, still ached for him.

They didn't speak much on the way to the club. When he parked, she turned to look at him. She wanted to thank him for the ride, and in doing so, hoped to work up the courage to ask if they could get together to talk.

"Someone's here," he said, looking over her shoulder before she could get a word out.

She turned to see. Any club employee would have pulled around to the back, but she recognized the van. "Cleaning crew. I forgot they came by in the mornings. Let's go around back. I don't want to disturb them."

"No problem." He started the car again and moved to park at the back.

She sensed something wasn't right the second she opened the door to get out. It started as a slight queasy feeling, but soon a horrible dread tinged with fear shook her body so violently she couldn't move.

"Tilly?" Keaton asked. "Is everything okay?"

"Yes," she lied and stepped outside, only to find the queasy sensation grew three hundred times worse. Her eyes scanned the area. "Is that door open?"

She tried telling herself it was simply the cleaning crew. That they had opened it. But they never cleaned the back. Granger refused to pay to have the employee only areas professionally cleaned.

"I think so." Keaton stood at her side. She hadn't realized he'd gotten out of the car. "Must be the people inside working. Looks like they left some laundry outside."

"We don't have laundry." Tilly recalled Raven's warning that something was going on and the shaking grew worse.

"I'm not sure what else it could be." Keaton walked toward the back door. After a few steps, he stopped and held out his arm to keep her from moving forward. But it was too late, she'd already seen. It wasn't laundry. It was Raven. And her throat had been cut.

Tilly screamed.

JADE

The mansion was massive and completely constructed of stone. It felt pretentious and over-the-top, and I couldn't help but think it looked out of place.

A car drove by on the street behind me, and I stopped myself from looking over my shoulder. The multitude of trees between the house and road provided both shelter and cover. As long as I remained still, I wouldn't be seen. I'd wanted to do this at night, but King said it had to be done during the day, and it had to be done today. Since I didn't have a death wish, I simply nodded and told him it was as good as done.

King hadn't said as much, but I knew he meant this errand as a test, and I had no intention of failing.

"Look for an old ivy covered arbor," I muttered, repeating his instructions. "Once you move it out of the way, you'll see a wooden door."

I saw exactly one ivy covered arbor in the garden. "Yeah, right." I snorted. "That sucker looks like it hasn't been moved since the Revolutionary War."

I listened a long minute for the sound of an approaching car or someone out for an afternoon stroll. Hearing nothing, I took a deep breath and lifted the arbor. It was surprisingly light and easily moved, and, just like he said, revealed a wooden door.

I smiled and checked to make sure my knife was easily accessible. This was going to be a cake walk.

CHAPTER 6

Keaton sat with his arms around Tilly, trying to shield her from the sight of her coworker, and letting her sob in disbelief while they waited for the police to arrive. He didn't remember seeing Tilly cry before, and though he initially felt a bit awkward holding her, it became more natural the longer she remained in his arms.

"I saw her two days ago," Tilly said, pulling back slightly. "She was perfectly fine. How could something like this happen?"

He didn't have any comforting words to offer, so he simply held her. The police should be arriving soon, he'd called them as soon as Tilly had been able to tell him who the dead woman was. The cleaning crew stood some distance away but close enough to see what was going on. They'd come running as soon as they heard Tilly scream and now watched in shock.

An unmarked car with flashing lights pulled up.

"Police are here," he whispered to Tilly. She sniffled once more and took a step back and out of his arms.

A woman got out of the car first. She was petite and had

her hair pulled back in a ponytail. But what primarily caught his attention was the confidence in her step and the way her eyes took in her surroundings. Her male partner glanced around the area quickly, but his steps were hesitant. The woman walked toward them and flashed her badge.

"I'm Officer Alyssa Adams. This is my partner, Officer Warren. We had a call about a body."

Tilly pointed to Raven. "It's Raven. Raven Todd. We work together."

"And you are?" Alyssa asked.

"Tilly Brock."

A flash of something flickered in Alyssa's eyes, but she didn't address it. Turning to him, she asked, "And you?"

"Keaton Benedict."

Alyssa nodded to her partner, who started making calls and turned back to the couple. "Tell me what happened."

Keaton let Tilly give a rundown of the day's events. By the time she'd finished, more people had arrived to process the scene.

"Did Raven mention anything about someone threatening her?" Alyssa asked.

"No." Tilly's forehead wrinkled. "But two nights ago, she mentioned she thought something was going on."

Alyssa frowned. "Did she say what?"

"Just that King, he's the club owner, was supposed to be coming by for a visit, and I remember thinking it strange because no one I know has ever seen or spoken to the man."

"King? I'll ask around." Alyssa looked toward where someone was taking pictures. "Okay. Thank you. Those are all the questions I have for the moment."

"Can I go?" Tilly asked.

"Yes, of course. Be sure to let me know if you remember anything."

Tilly thanked her after they all exchanged information. Keaton wasn't sure how long it would take to process the scene, but Officer Adams had told them they could leave, and he wasn't about to stick around. "Let's go," he whispered and ushered her back to his car.

Once inside and shielded somewhat from the crime scene, he turned to ask her where she wanted to go. She looked so vulnerable huddled in his front seat. So many questions ran through his head. He assumed she didn't have a car, which meant she either walked everywhere or took public transportation. He didn't like it, but obviously, there wasn't much he could do short of buying her a car. Based on her reaction to the insurance policy, she'd go ape shit if he bought her a car. He would think of something, though. There was no other choice.

KEATON STAYED with her all day, rarely leaving her side. Since she hadn't been to the grocery store in over a week, he ordered delivery from an Italian place for lunch and sushi for dinner. Tilly didn't have much of an appetite, but she ate anyway, knowing she had to.

Throughout the day, Raven's death would hit her suddenly, and she'd find herself crying. It didn't seem possible Raven was gone forever, and Tilly didn't know how she'd face going back to work knowing she would never be there again.

By late afternoon, she'd finally stopped crying so often and sat next to Keaton on her threadbare couch. He'd found an old James Bond movie playing on the TV, but neither of them were paying very much attention to what was happening on screen.

She hated he knew how low she'd fallen in life, hated he was sitting on her couch that had been covered and recovered so many times, she had no idea what its original color had been. But the fact remained, she was very glad he'd stayed.

"I don't know what I'd have done today without you." She turned to get a better look at him. "Thank you for staying."

"I would never leave you alone after what you went through. And besides," he added with a grin, "I like your company."

"Now I know you're lying. I've been the worst company today. I haven't done anything other than cry."

"I've missed you for eight years, you think a few tears are going to chase me away?"

She dropped her head. "I missed you, too."

It felt strange to acknowledge out loud, but it was the truth.

"You did?"

"Mmm." She nodded but didn't look up.

He covered her hand with his. "Hey, look at me." He waited until she did. "If I'd known you were in town, I'd have found you sooner. I'm still mad as hell Kipling knew and never told me. I owe him a kick in the ass."

Tilly eyes flew open. It took her a minute to realize she was on the couch with her head on Keaton's shoulder. James Bond was fighting a bad guy on the muted television, and the only noise was a sleeping Keaton's soft and steady breathing. What made her wake up? She distinctly remembered hearing something in the second before she became fully awake.

She reached for her phone, but there were no notifications. With a groan, she noted it was after five in the morning. Her back ached from spending the night on her couch, and she was certain her hair looked frightening. Her movements caused Keaton to stir. He gave her a lazy smile.

"Hey." He sat up. "What time is it?"

"After five."

"Shit." He ran his hands through his hair. "I didn't mean to fall asleep like that."

"It's okay. Maybe not the most comfortable way to spend the night, but obviously we were both more tired than we realized."

"Obviously," he said. "But I bet neither one of us will be able to go back to sleep. How about we freshen up and I take you out for breakfast? The Biscuit Shack is open, and we'll probably beat the crowd."

He must have expected her to decline because he wasn't able to hide his look of shock when she agreed. She bit back a laugh and told him he could use the bathroom first.

She didn't spend too much time getting ready. They were just going to The Biscuit Shack, a small local joint open only for breakfast but made biscuits so delicious it was always packed. As she was trying to tame her hair, Raven's murder hit her anew and a fresh wave of grief washed over her.

"You ready?" Concern and worry filled Keaton's eyes when she walked back into the living room.

She nodded. For some reason, being with Keaton lessened the sharp edge of her grief. He must have picked up on her mood change because he was smiling as he unlocked and opened the door. A flash of red caught her eye, and she looked down. One of the twin's lifeless bodies blocked her way.

Like Raven, her throat had been cut, and Tilly's free hand flew of its own accord to her own neck. This wasn't a coincidence. This was a warning.

CHAPTER 7

"This is twice in as many days that you've called to report a body," Officer Adams said as if somehow both women were dead because of them.

Tilly started to say something, but Keaton stopped her by answering first. "We're not saying anything without a lawyer present."

Officer Adams cocked one eyebrow. "Noted."

"Doesn't that make us look guilty?" Tilly whispered to Keaton.

"No, it makes us look smart."

Tilly sighed and stood from her couch. She wanted to go outside, but the crime scene team she recognized from the day before was blocking her doorway. She thought she would have felt something over the death of another coworker, but all she felt was numb.

From outside a commotion began to stir. Keaton stood.

"I don't give a fuck. I'm going in," a familiar voice said from outside. Tilly looked at Keaton in question, and he nodded.

Seconds later, Kipling stood in her apartment with arms

crossed. "Looks like we're all getting an early start today." It was only a minute or two after six and Kipling was already dressed for work. Suit. Tie. Italian leather shoes. Did the man own a pair of jeans?

"Who are you?" Alyssa asked.

Kipling turned and gave the police officer a frank look over. "Kipling Benedict of Benedict Industries." He shot her a smile. "And you are?"

"Officer Alyssa Adams and this is Officer Warren," Alyssa replied. "We're looking into the death of Mindy Jackson." At Kipling's nod, Alyssa shifted her focus back to Tilly and Keaton. "We've heard there was an altercation between Keaton, Tilly, and Mindy a few nights ago at the club where the women worked."

Keaton shook his head. "I, uh, don't know if *altercation* is the right word."

"Keaton." Kipling said in the low but dangerous voice he had. "Shut your fucking mouth and keep it closed until Derrick gets here."

"Or he could answer a few questions and we'll get out of your hair," Alyssa said.

"No one says anything, damn it."

They all turned to see who had spoken.

"Our attorney," Keaton whispered to Tilly as the man in question entered the crowded room. He was short and overweight, and though it was early in the day, already sweating

"Derrick Gains," the lawyer addressed the two officers. "I represent the Benedict family, and we're not answering anything." He looked around the room, his gaze landed on Tilly. "Who are you?"

"Tilly Brock. I live here."

Derrick looked from her to Kipling, who gave a slight

nod. At once, the lawyer snapped his head back to the two officers. "She's my client, too."

Tilly's mouth fell open in shock and though she closed it just was fast, the move hadn't gone unnoticed. Kipling had been watching her. He winked when their eyes met.

The male officer who had been silent through the entire exchange, stood. "Come on," he said to Alyssa. "We're not going to get anything here."

Alyssa wasn't happy to be leaving, that much was clear. "I suggest neither of you leave town," she told Keaton and Tilly. To Kipling, she simply said, "I'll be in touch."

Kipling saluted her and appeared to be watching her ass as she left.

Everyone held their breath until the two officers left. Derrick looked at Keaton. "Want to tell me what's been going on?"

Keaton took a deep breath and told him everything he knew, everything he remembered, and everything that happened after they left the club up to this morning. Derrick made notes, then turned to Tilly for her side. When they both finished, he clasped his hands. "We'll get statements from everyone, and that should be it."

He stayed a few minutes more, mostly making small talk, and it wasn't until Derrick left that there was a noticeable change in Kipling's demeanor. Keaton's older brother took a deep breath and rolled his shoulders. He closed his eyes and sighed, but when he opened them, he was all smiles.

Tilly wanted to smile, but she couldn't. How could she smile when Raven and Mindy never would smile again?

Keaton seemed to pick up on her mood because he was frowning, too. "You okay, Tilly?"

She shook her had. "It's just sinking in that Mindy's

gone. I mean, I didn't like her, but I didn't want her dead." She dropped her head into her hand. "Who could do this?"

Keaton put his arm around her. "I don't know, but I'll do anything I can to help because it makes me sick to my stomach, too. How could someone I talked with days ago be dead? Even more upsetting is the thought that something I saw or heard might be a clue, but how do I know?"

"Right?" Tilly agreed. "What if there was something and I'm not able to remember it? Even more sickening is the thought that it happened outside my door." She tightened her hands into fists. "And I can't help thinking, was it Mindy or me they were after?"

Keaton's lips tightened into a thin line. "Why would you be a target?"

"I don't know, but I have to think about it, don't I?"

He didn't look too happy with her statement, and she expected him to argue with her, but Kipling's phone rang and conversation stopped when he cursed as he looked at the display. "Hello, Mr. Germain," he said, answering while at the same time keeping his gaze locked on Keaton. "Yes, I understand. No, there's nothing to worry about. Yes, he has an alibi. Of course. No offense taken. I'd have done the same. Yes, sir. We're looking forward to her staying with us."

"The hell we are," Keaton mumbled under his breath.

Tilly sucked in a breath, and Keaton turned his attention back to her.

"Are you okay?"

She hadn't meant to be so loud, but hearing Kipling talk to Mr. Germain brought home the fact that there were people she might have to interact with even though she'd thought she'd never have to see or speak to them again.

"Are you and Elise...?" She didn't ask the question, hoping he would see what she wanted to know.

He shook his head. "There's nothing between me and Elise. She would like for there to be. Her parents would like for there to be. But it's not going to happen. Elise is a beautiful woman and I'm sure she'll make some guy a wonderful wife, but it won't be me."

"Did your parents want you two together?" she asked.

"It's mostly her father. He thinks our business portfolios would match up, but Mom and Dad never would have wanted me to marry someone for business gain." He grimaced. "That memo hasn't made it to the Germain house, though. I've been selected in much the same way you would decide on a horse to breed. Good bloodlines. Sturdy stock. Not too bad to look at. Loaded. Yup, I'll do for a husband."

The whole thing sounded clinical and cold. "Kinda makes me glad my parents didn't have much money." *After,* she could have added, but didn't.

"The bad part is, her dad still doesn't see the fruitlessness of it." He hesitated a second before adding, "She's spending the summer at Benedict House."

"I thought she went to Yale or Harvard or something."

"Harvard."

"When's she arriving?"

He shot Kipling a look.

"Monday," Kipling replied.

"Day after tomorrow, Monday?" Tilly asked.

Keaton shot his older brother a look. "Unfortunately."

"How long is she staying?" she asked, even though she had a bad feeling she knew.

"The whole damn summer. She's *interning* at a law office."

She tilted her head. "Something about the way you said that makes me think you don't believe it."

"I can't picture Elise as an attorney. She's been groomed from the crib to be a trophy wife."

It sounded awful coming from Keaton's lips, but Tilly knew he was telling the truth. Years ago, whenever she'd spent the night at Elise's house, her mother was always on her to do this and act that way and not to ever do XYZ. Tilly remembered thinking how fortunate she felt that her mother didn't expect her to live following a bunch of worthless rules.

She'd told Elise that once, but her friend had denied it and said that her mother wanted to ensure she grew up to be a proper Southern lady. Tilly snorted and said it sounded boring as hell. Elise hadn't taken that very well. Looking back, they probably wouldn't have been friends if their fathers hadn't both worked for the Benedicts.

"She probably went to Harvard for her MRS degree," Tilly said.

"Without question," Keaton agreed.

There was a lull in the conversation and, with it, Tilly realized how quiet it had grown outside. She stood to walk to the front window right as someone knocked on the front door.

She opened it to find Officer Adams. "Can I help you, Officer?"

Alyssa shook her head. "No, Ms. Brock. I just wanted to let you know we were finished and will be leaving. I'll let you know if I have further questions for you." She handed her card to Tilly. "And here's my card if you remember anything that might help the case."

Tilly put the card in her pocket. "Thank you."

Once Alyssa left and Tilly closed the door, Kipling stood.

"I'll get out of your hair, too. Keaton, are you staying here or coming home?"

Keaton turned to her. "Why don't you come stay at Benedict House?"

As much as she would like to, she didn't want to be around Elise. Though they had been close at one point, they hadn't talked in years. From what she understood from Keaton, Elise wasn't the same person she'd been then, and he'd hinted she'd become quite the snob. Add to that the fact Elise wanted Keaton for her own? Hard pass.

"I'll stay here," she said, "and probably take a nap."

"I'll stay, too," Keaton said.

"No, I'm sure you have other things to do."

He looked like he was going to argue, but she stopped him by walking to him and slipping her arms around him. She was vaguely aware of Kipling leaving. "But if you like, you can take me to dinner. I have something my mom gave me, and I want to see if you recognize it."

"Sounds intriguing. You're on, but call me if you need anything," Keaton whispered against her cheek. "Anything at all."

"Okay," she said.

He kissed her cheek, and she wondered if telling him not to stay was the stupidest thing she'd ever done.

JADE

I knew something was up the second King walked into my room. He very rarely sought me out, and it was never a good thing when he did.

I put down the knife I'd been sharpening. "Something wrong, sir?"

"I heard good reports about your work."

His praise was rare and a flicker of warmth started to fill the dark and empty places inside me.

"You aren't totally worthless, after all," he said with a laugh, and I was once more cold to my very soul.

"Thank you, sir," I whispered.

He nodded toward the knives in front of me. "Bring them and follow me. You need more practice."

My stomach flipped in revolt, but I did as I was told.

CHAPTER 8

Tilly turned off her cell as soon as Keaton left. There was no one she wanted to speak with, and it felt as if the buzz of incoming alerts never stopped. Her current plan was to stay sequestered inside her apartment for at least the next eight hours. Maybe by then the reporters would be gone.

She plopped into her couch and hugged a pillow to her chest. When had everything gone so crazy? In just a few days, so much had changed.

Restless, she got up and paced to the window; a few reporters lingered in the parking lot. With a sigh, she turned on her computer and opened the spreadsheet she kept her budget on. She did the math three times. Even if she only ate beans and rice, the longest she could go without working was a week at best. She didn't want to go back to the club, but she doubted she could find another waitressing job. With her name and picture all over the news, she didn't think anyone would hire her.

What she needed to do was figure out what the deal was with the key her mother gave her. The most logical assumption was it opened a safety deposit box at a bank. But which one? There were so many in the Charleston area, and she didn't know with any certainty that the key belonged to a bank in the first place. She planned to show it to Keaton after dinner to see if he could tell her anything about it.

She reached for her phone and turned it on, unsurprised when her screen filled with missed calls. Two were from Keaton, and, as expected, numerous were from numbers she didn't recognize, and a few were simply listed as *unknown*. Interestingly enough, there was only one voicemail.

She hit play, expecting to hear Keaton, but it wasn't his voice that filled her ear. It was a robotic sounding, maniacal rough voice.

"You should have stayed where you were."

She deleted it with a shiver. Damn the media spreading her name all over the place and turning the day into a game for perverts and other creepers. It wasn't a secret who she was, and it had only been a matter of time before someone asked why the hell she came back. The phone rang again and flashed UNKNOWN. Best to let it go to voicemail. If it was important enough, they'd leave a message.

KEATON TRIED CALLING Tilly for the second time from the house landline after his shower, but it once again went to her voicemail. More than likely, she was being bombarded and had turned off her phone. He didn't bother to leave a message since it wouldn't be too long before he took her to dinner.

He stood in the hallway and looked at his watch,

wondering how long was an acceptable period of time to wait before heading back to Tilly's.

Kipling walked by him and chuckled. "Come talk with me for a minute. Then you can go see her."

"That transparent, am I?"

"Slightly."

Keaton's phone buzzed with an incoming text. *Tilly. Finally.* But when he pulled the phone out of his pocket, it was an unfamiliar number and his blood ran cold at what had been sent.

That thief's offspring better watch her step.

Twenty minutes later, Keaton stood at the doorway of Tilly's apartment. There were a few reporters in the parking lot and they all said they hadn't seen anyone leave or enter her place. But that didn't erase the fact Tilly still wasn't answering her phone. Even if she'd turned it off to avoid reporters, surely she would have turned it back on to check for voicemails.

A tiny trickle of fear twisted in his chest even as he knocked on her door. He told himself he was being ridiculous, that she would open the door and he'd feel foolish. She'd welcome him inside and they'd share a laugh over his overreaction.

Except she wasn't opening the door.

"Tilly!" He banged harder. "Tilly, it's Keaton. Open up and let me know you're okay."

Still nothing from within.

He looked under the welcome mat, but of course, there was no key to be found. There were no potted plants and the mailboxes were located across the parking lot. Frustrated, he tried calling her again.

Nothing.

Damn it.

He ran his fingers through his hair, telling himself to calm down and think about the situation rationally. No one had entered or exited the front door. His head shot up.

The front door.

Was there a backdoor?

Seconds later, he made it to the backside of the apartments. There was indeed a backdoor. Without thinking, he tried the knob. It wasn't locked.

He stood frozen in place for several seconds, fighting not to give into the fear threatening to consume him. He couldn't lose Tilly. Not after they'd found each other after so many years. He had to find her, and she had to be okay. There was no other option.

He took a step into her kitchen, closing his eyes to pray he wouldn't find her dead on the floor with a slit throat. His fingers wrapped around the phone in his pocket, ready to call 911.

"Get the fuck out of my house!"

His eyes flew open. "Tilly?"

"Keaton?" she asked, appearing from a nearby hallway, and sliding off the headphones she'd been wearing. "What are you doing and how did you get inside?"

Keaton left the phone in his pocket. "Why the hell is your door unlocked?"

"I just came back inside, and I couldn't lock it because my hands were full." She placed a hand on her chest. "I was on my way back from the kitchen and saw a shadow moving. I was scared out of my mind thinking someone had broken in."

He took a deep breath, ready to rip into her until she understood how stupid she'd been to leave her door unlocked and promised to never do it again. But when he looked at her, shaking with her hand still on her chest, all he could think was she was okay. She was fine. And he realized he do anything in his power to keep her that way. Without knowing what he was doing, he crossed the floor, took her in his arms and crushed his lips to hers.

It wasn't a gentle kiss. It was raw and rough, and he didn't care. All he cared about was that she was in his arms safe and alive. She wrapped her arms around him and gave back to him as much as he gave her.

They were both breathing heavily when they pulled back.

He ran his hands over her hair, looking deep into her eyes. "Leave your door unlocked again like that and I'll pull you across my lap and wear your ass out."

Desire and need flashed across her face in the second it took to school her features.

She wrinkled her nose. "You and what army?"

He didn't tell her that he didn't need an army. "You weren't answering your phone, and I got a strange text. I came over here, you didn't answer your door, and when I made it to the back, I found your door unlocked."

He hadn't planned to tell her about the text he received because he didn't want to worry her unnecessarily. He'd just shot that plan straight to hell. Tilly looked several shades paler.

"What?" he asked. "What's wrong?"

"I had a strange voicemail."

"Do you still have it?"

"No, I deleted it. It said something like 'You should have stayed away.'"

Keaton was so stunned, he couldn't say anything, and Tilly paled even further. "Oh my god," she whispered. "What if they're after me? The person who killed Raven and Mindy."

"We can't ignore the possibility." It pained him to even think it, much less confirm out loud.

"Oh my god," she repeated.

"Tilly," he said to get her attention. "Please think about staying at Benedict House. It's safer."

"Okay. I'll give it some thought." She sniffled and added, "I turned my phone off because all of the people calling me. Then, I went to my neighbor's because I stress bake, and I went out the back way because of the reporters."

He cocked an eyebrow a her. "Two people you work with were murdered. You got a threatening phone call. And you decided to go next door and *bake*?"

"I had to do something. The only other option was to sit here and drive myself crazy over every little sound I heard." She led him into the kitchen. "I haven't been to the store lately, and I didn't feel like going today. When that happens, Ms. O'Donald next door lets me use her kitchen and supplies. She's in her nineties and good company. Plus, I like to keep an eye on her."

When that happens, she'd said. He had a feeling she couldn't afford to buy groceries, especially based on what he remembered from her kitchen. And, based on her words, this wasn't the first time she'd been in that position. Damn it, why wouldn't she take the insurance money? She was seriously going to let pride keep her from eating?

"What did you bake today?" he asked to change the subject.

Even as she started rattling off the things she had baking next door, he couldn't stop thinking about her not being able to afford groceries. It was grossly unfair, he had all the money he'd ever need and she had to scrimp pennies to buy food.

"How about I take you to the store to buy groceries?" he asked. If she insisted on staying here, he would at least ensure she had something to eat.

"No, that's okay." She glanced at the clock on her oven. "I need to check on the muffins in five minutes. Want to go with me?"

After thinking he'd almost lost her, there wasn't a force on earth strong enough to keep him away from her.

"As long as we go out and come back in the front doors."

"Deal."

"And you promise me you have something to eat other than sweets."

"I promise."

THIRTY MINUTES LATER, Tilly and Keaton sat at her small kitchen table, eating muffins and drinking ice tea.

Keaton reached for his third muffin. "You should open a bakery."

She laughed and refilled his tea. "I only stress bake; I don't think I have it in me to do it as an occupation."

"Shame," he said, mouth full of muffin.

It was amazing how easy it was to be around him. She'd have thought it would be awkward, given not only their history, but that of their fathers as well. But it wasn't. It was almost as if the years they were apart melted away. Then she'd catch a glimpse of him watching her and his eyes were so intense, she swore she felt it all the way to her toes.

And the way he kissed her? Uh, yeah. That certainly hadn't happened when they were kids.

"What about you," she asked. "Now that you've graduated are you going to take your place at the helm of Benedict Industries?"

"Not if I can help it."

"Really? Why? I thought it was like a Benedict rule or something."

"I don't mind working for Benedict Industries, but not in the capacity Kipling wants."

She tilted her head. "I'm not sure I understand."

He looked a bit uneasy as if he didn't want to explain. "I spent the summers after my sophomore and junior years in India working to bring water to remote villages."

To hear that this wealthy man the world wrote off as a playboy spent summers in India helping the impoverished endeared him to her all the more. "Wow, had no idea."

"I don't talk about it a lot."

She nodded. Not only had he spent summers trying to make the world a better place, he kept everything about it private. "How does water in India fit in with Benedict Industries?"

"I want to open up a division within the company, one that deals with giving back. First to Charleston, then South Carolina, and to keep spreading outward. It seems wrong to have all that money and not give back to the community. There are too many people in need. I can't help them all, but hopefully I can make a small impact."

"You're amazing," she whispered in awe at the man he'd become.

"You flatter me. I'm sure all you have to do is pick up the society page and you'll get an eyeful of how not amazing I am."

She knew that for a fact even if she never read them. And he was right, there were plenty of them. He was one of the Benedict brothers, after all. All three were regarded as prime picking and the media loved them.

"But those don't represent the entirety of you," she said.

"They represent enough."

"You'll never do great things until you believe you can do them."

CHAPTER 9

"Where are we going for dinner?" she asked hours later as they walked to his car.

"There's a new seafood place near the office. I can't remember the name, but Kipling went on and on about how good it was, and he's a seafood snob."

She knew of the place. It was upscale, supposedly ridiculously delicious, and nothing she could afford.

"What?" he asked, catching her side eye at him. He opened the car door for her. "I want to take you somewhere nice."

"You know you don't have to."

"You fed me all those baked goods. Let me do this."

She knew he was wealthy, but she also knew he wasn't trying to impress her with his wealth. In his mind, he was taking her to a nice seafood restaurant. It was her hang up that it cost so much. If it didn't bother him, it shouldn't bother her.

"Okay," she said, as he pulled out of the parking lot. "But next date, I'm in charge."

"There's going to be a next date? We haven't even finished this one yet," he teased. "Damn, I'm good."

"Don't let it go to your head," she said with a laugh.

If it had been another man of Keaton's means taking her out, she would assume he was taking her to such an expensive place to try to get in her pants. But she trusted Keaton and knew he wasn't like that. He simply wanted to do nice things for her. It felt nice to be taken care of.

They arrived at the restaurant and the hostess led them to a relatively private table with a waterfront view. Keaton ordered a bottle of wine, and she tried not to be too obvious as she took in her surroundings. The restaurant was made from an old fish market, but had been redone with rich woods and new brick. She didn't even want to look at the menu, afraid that if she did, she wouldn't be able to keep the cost from bothering her.

Keaton, however, had no such issues. He looked up at her over the top of his menu. "Know what you want already?"

"No," she said. "I'll let you order for me."

"You trust me that much?"

She knew he asked it as a joke, but her reply was completely serious. "Yes."

He held her gaze for a long minute. "I'm going to beat Kipling's ass for not telling me he had been in contact with you."

Whatever else he was going to say was interrupted by the waitress coming to take their order. He ordered them both a cup of she-crab soup and the catch of the day.

"I'm on a mission to find the best she-crab soup in the city," he said. "I haven't tried here yet."

"That makes sense. I was wondering why anyone would order soup when it's so hot outside."

He cocked his head to the side. "It does sound a bit absurd, doesn't it?"

"Absurd is how unreal it is this is really real." She laughed. "And how many *reals* were in that sentence."

When they were young, she'd been captivated by his good looks and kind personality. But as the date progressed, she saw that the older Keaton was so much more. He was easy to talk to, intelligent, and compassionate. Most guys she dated only wanted to talk about themselves, but Keaton wanted to know how she felt and what she thought. It made her feel cherished and important. By the time they'd finished dinner, she feared her heart wasn't at all safe around the youngest Benedict.

THE RIDE back to her apartment was passed in a comfortable silence. She'd expected the date to go well, but Keaton was simply amazing. Now, she was trying to figure out how to invite him inside without seeming too desperate.

When they were kids, Keaton's favorite cake had been a ten-layer chocolate. She didn't start baking to relieve stress until her mother got sick, but when she started, the first cake she taught herself to make was a ten-layer chocolate.

And there was a freshly baked one sitting right on top of her kitchen island.

"Come inside?" she asked when he'd parked in front of her building. "I have cake. One I didn't tell you about before."

He reached over and brushed her cheek. "Is that what you said you wanted to show me? Cake?"

"No, that's something different."

"How can I turn down cake and something different?

Don't touch that door." He hopped out of his side of the car. "I'll get it."

She sat back in her seat. Even though she believed his parents had been tricked by someone into thinking her dad had stolen from them, and even though it'd hurt her that they never questioned it, the one thing she could say was they did a fine job instilling manners into their boys.

She knew the reputation of the Benedict brothers; she wasn't a fool, but that was only on the surface. She had a feeling not many people knew the real men underneath the playboy facade.

They walked together to her apartment. She couldn't describe why or how, but she felt like something was off. When they made it about halfway, the skin on the back of her neck prickled. She stopped and looked over her shoulder.

"You okay?" Keaton asked, his gaze following hers. "Did you see something?"

"No, I just feel odd. It's probably nothing." She strained her ears; were those footsteps nearby? Were they coming closer or farther away?

"How so?"

How could she explain it to him if she couldn't understand it herself? "Something feels off."

He looked over the parking lot and frowned. "Do you see anything that looks out of place? A strange car? Anything?"

She walked closer to him. "No, but I feel like I'm being watched."

They didn't say anything else as they continued, and the feeling only grew worse. In fact, by the time they reached her door, her hands were trembling so hard, she dropped her keys.

Keaton reached down to get them. "Are you sure you didn't see anything?"

He didn't give the keys back to her, but took them in hand to unlock the door himself. He turned the key to unlock the door and his frown deepened. "It's not locked?"

Fear spiked through her chest. "What? Are you sure? I know I locked it."

"I know you did. I watched you." He twisted the handle. "It's definitely unlocked. Does anyone have a key?"

Relief washed over her body. "Yes, my neighbor Ms. O'Donald. She probably needed her cake pans back."

He nodded. "Okay, but you seriously need to consider taking the key away from her if she can't remember to lock up when she leaves."

"Agreed." Tilly nodded but wasn't sure what she was going to do. Ms. O'Donald was ninety-three. Sometimes, she forgot things. But what if it wasn't Ms. O'Donald?

Keaton pushed the door open and stopped. "Oh, fuck."

CHAPTER 10

Tilly's apartment was a total wreck.

Furniture was overturned and slashed through. Mirrors and picture frames were broken with shards of glass littering the floor. Worst of all was the WHORE written in red along the far wall of her living room.

Behind him, Tilly gasped. He turned and took her in his arms and as he did, he felt her resolve return. She took a deep breath and pushed back, her eyes darting around the room. "Who the hell would have done this and how did they get in?"

"We need to call the police and wait downstairs." Keaton led her out of the apartment as he talked. "I don't think whoever did this is still around, but we can't be too sure."

She didn't argue with him, and by the time they'd made it back to his car, he'd already called the police. It wasn't long before flashing lights signaled their arrival. Once again, it was Alyssa and her partner.

"Mr. Benedict. Ms. Brock," Alyssa said, coming toward them.

Keaton and Tilly spoke to Alyssa and told her what they'd found in the apartment. Alyssa sent her partner up to check everything out. It wasn't too long until he came back down. He spoke briefly with Alyssa and then walked to the car to make a phone call.

"No one's in there now," Alyssa said. "You'll need to go through and see if anything has been stolen, but it looks like the place was just trashed."

"Why would anyone do that?" Tilly asked.

"I don't know," Alyssa said. "If it's the guy who killed Raven and Mindy, he broke pattern. He didn't do this to either of their places. Of course, that doesn't rule him out."

Which wasn't what Keaton wanted to hear. He'd wanted Alyssa to say that, of course, this wasn't the work of the killer. And since she couldn't say that, it was even more imperative that Tilly move in with him.

Tilly thought for a few seconds before saying, "I had a prank call yesterday. Whoever it was said I should have never moved here."

"I received a text message yesterday saying Tilly needed to watch herself," he added.

"You should have called me," Alyssa said. "If either of you get another message, I want you to let me know. Immediately."

They agreed, and Alyssa told them they were free to go back into the apartment, but to let her know if anything was missing.

Keaton waited until the two cops left before placing a hand on her shoulder. "Ready?"

"No." She looked toward her door. "But I don't think I'll ever be completely ready, so I might as well go now."

Her grit and determination amazed him, and he leaned

84

over to give her a quick kiss. "Let's go see if anything's missing, and then I'd like for you to pack a bit and come with me to Benedict House."

"I'm not sure...."

"I don't like the idea of you staying here. It's not safe."

"Then I'll get a..." she didn't finish her sentence and he winced as he realized she probably didn't have the funds for a hotel room.

"Tilly, please." He'd beg if he had to, knowing he wouldn't feel comfortable with her anywhere other than Benedict House.

It was on her lips to say no, he could see it in her eyes, but then her expression softened. "Keaton."

"Please." he repeated, softer. "I need you safe. I've only just found you again." He lowered his head so his lips almost brushed her ear and he delighted at her shiver. "Please."

Some part of him knew he was playing unfairly. She was vulnerable, and he was pulling at her emotions, but he didn't care. He'd meant every word of it, and he'd do far more to keep her safe. No matter what, she was staying with him tonight.

She sighed deeply, but tilted her head up and whispered, "Yes."

Even though they'd seen the mess earlier, it wasn't any easier the second time. As heart wrenching as it was for him to see all her things scattered and broken, he could only imagine how it made her feel.

One glance at her told him she was putting on a brave front. She walked stoically through the tattered living room, seeming to note each item with a nod of her head. He followed quietly, aghast at how much damage had been done. Hell, there wasn't one picture unbroken or one unlashed cushion. Even her clothing had been pulled from her bedroom and scattered throughout her hallway. He wasn't sure there was enough untouched clothing for her to pack in an overnight bag. Heaven alone knew what kind of damage they'd find in the bathroom.

A muffled sob from the kitchen caught his attention, and he hurried to catch up with her. He hadn't realized she'd moved ahead of him that far. She stood by the kitchen island, her face in her hands, sobbing.

"Tilly?" He came to a halt behind her and placed a hand on her shoulder.

She turned around, and her red, wet eyes hurt his heart. When he found out who did this, and he would, they were going to pay. He'd see to it himself.

"They ruined your cake," she said, pointing to the floor, which he now noticed was covered with yellow cake pieces and smears of light chocolate icing. "Your ten-layer chocolate cake."

She buried her head in his chest and cried. Not knowing what else to do, he simply held her, stroking her back and murmuring that it would be okay. The entire time, hoping and praying he was right, but very afraid he was telling her lies.

TILLY DECIDED Keaton must think she was an idiot. Her entire apartment was trashed, and she fell apart because of a *cake?* Though to be honest, she'd been pretty close to losing it since the first step into her apartment. It was just seeing the cake all over the floor that finally pushed her over the edge. The cake she'd baked because once upon a time it had been his favorite, and she wanted to do something special for him.

And now, it was smashed all over her floor.

She pushed back from him and wiped her eyes. "I'm sorry. I'm okay now."

"What in the world are you apologizing for?" he asked. "I believe coming home to find your apartment ransacked is a perfectly acceptable reason to be upset."

She straightened her back. "I need to clean this up."

"No." He held out an arm to stop her. "Do a quick look around to see if anything's missing, grab an overnight bag, and we're going to Benedict House."

"I can't just leave this like it is."

"Yes, you can."

"No. I can't."

"You can and you are," his voice had changed. He probably wasn't even aware of it, but he'd taken on the *You'll do as I say because I said so* tone she'd heard Kipling use before. Most likely it was embedded in the Benedict DNA. "I'll send over a cleaning crew tomorrow."

"A cleaning crew? Keaton—"

He put a finger to her lips. "Check to see if anything's missing. Pack an overnight bag. We can argue about cleanup later. I don't feel comfortable with you being here any longer than you have to be."

His words had the desired effect and she looked over her shoulder. No one was here now, but did that mean they were really gone or they were just hiding and couldn't be seen? Without another word, she checked on the few valuables she had.

Her laptop screen had been smashed as well as her TV, but the secret hiding place she kept her mother's few pieces of jewelry and the key was undisturbed. She lifted the small velvet bag from between her boxsprings and mattress and looked around for an overnight bag.

She found one in the hall and forced herself to turn off her emotions while she packed. She could do this, just put clothes in a bag. She didn't even look to see if they were messed up, rather she shoved anything nearby into the bag.

"I don't think you'll need the puffer jacket," Keaton said, gently removing it from the bag. "How about you go gather what you need from the bathroom, and I'll finish up in here."

With a nod, she walked away, doing her best to shut herself off from what she was actually doing and instead focused on what she needed. Toothbrush. In the toilet. Surely the Benedicts had a spare. Makeup. Dumped out across the countertop. With a sound that wasn't quite a laugh, she decided she didn't need anything in the bathroom anyway.

"I need to borrow a toothbrush," she told Keaton as she walked back into her bedroom.

He looked up from zipping up her bag. "We can handle that. You ready?"

She took one last look around what a few hours ago had been her safe haven, her home, and sighed. "Yes."

She was not going to cry again. She was not.

"Hey," Keaton tugged the strap of the bag over his shoulder and pulled her to his chest. "It's going to be okay. I promise."

"How do you know? Look at this." The wide sweep of her arm encompassed the whole of the apartment.

With one finger, he lifted her chin so she had no choice but to look into his eyes. "Because there are two of us now. And together we can handle it."

She wanted so desperately to believe him. Truly she did.

But they had only reconnected days ago after spending years apart. Emotionally, she couldn't afford to put all her eggs in his basket; it was too risky. Her heart couldn't handle losing him twice.

But as she looked into his strange brown eyes, she knew she'd offend him if she spoke her doubts, so instead she swallowed them, smiled, and said, "Okay."

"Good," he said even though he probably knew she wouldn't argue with him. "It's settled then. We'll get you to Benedict House, have a good night's rest, and the cleaning crew will come by in the morning." With a hand on her lower back, he led her to the door.

"What's it like?" she asked.

"What's what like?"

She waited while he locked the door. "To speak a word and have the whole world do your bidding?"

He looked momentarily stunned as if he hadn't heard right or maybe it was that he never realized that was what happened. She feared it was the first and she'd gone and offended him anyway.

But he smiled the easy smile that always seemed to make her heart flutter *just so,* and said, "Pretty damn good, actually."

His answer was so unexpected, she broke out into laughter. Still smiling, he took her hand. "Let's get out of here."

She couldn't agree more. And even though the apartment was a wreck and she was moving temporarily into a house she wasn't completely comfortable living in, his hand felt perfect and right wrapped around hers. It didn't escape her attention he was once more protecting her in that caring way of his. Even with everything going on and with all the questions surrounding her apartment and who trashed it, her heart still felt light because she knew Keaton would keep her safe.

Their levity was shorter than expected, however, because when they reached his car, all four tires had been slashed.

CHAPTER 11

"*A*re you calling the police?" Tilly asked him as he pulled out his phone.

"Yes," he said. "Part of me believes it won't do any good, but in this case, I think it's best to err on the side of caution." He cocked an eyebrow. "Do you feel the same?"

"I trust Officer Adams," she told him. "I'm not sure I feel the same about her partner yet. But there's something different about her."

Keaton nodded and started dialing. "I saw it, too."

They didn't have to wait long for Alyssa to show back up. This time she arrived without her partner. She explained that he was writing the report from earlier in the evening. Something in her tone of voice and the look in her eye gave Tilly the impression she was relieved he'd stayed behind.

Tilly and Keaton stood off to the side while she looked over the car and made a phone call. It seemed to Tilly that she took her time and was surprised when the officer waved them over to her instead of coming to them.

"Did you find something, Officer?" Keaton asked.

"I'm going to be honest with you both," Alyssa said, "because I think it's the right thing to do and because this could potentially be a dangerous situation."

What the hell? Beside her, she felt Keaton tense, and she knew he hadn't liked Alyssa's response either.

"Officially," Alyssa said. "It is the position of the Charleston PD that the break in and the tires are not related to the recent kidnappings and murders."

"And unofficially?" Tilly asked while giving a sideways glance to Keaton. He looked seconds away from exploding.

"Unofficially," Alyssa said. "I find everything to be too coincidental. I don't believe in coincidence. Come here." She walked to the back tires and waited for them. When they had, she pointed to the slash. "See this? It's not the sort of slash we normally see. Based on my experience, it looks more like it was made with an elite type service knife."

"What are you saying?" Keaton asked.

"I think we're seeing a break in pattern because there are multiple people involved: the mastermind and his minions. I'm also saying you should be extremely vigilant about your safety. Don't take unneeded risks. Be on the lookout for anything suspicious. That sort of thing."

ALYSSA WAITED until they'd called a cab and were picked up before she left. On the way, Keaton sent Kipling a text telling him he'd be home in ten minutes, that Tilly was coming to stay, and that he'd explain everything when he got there. Kipling sent back a simple *Okay*.

His older brother waited outside as they pulled up. "Maggie is putting some things for Tilly in the guest room closest to yours." Kipling said to Keaton after greeting Tilly.

"Perfect," Keaton replied.

"Come in and sit down." He led them into the living room and motioned toward a couch. Keaton took a seat and pulled Tilly down by his side. "You look like you need a drink. Tell me what's going on while I pour."

Keaton knew he'd given his older brother hell while they were growing up. Heck, he still liked to push his buttons on occasion, but it was times like this when he wondered what he'd do without him. Kipling was often viewed as cold and ruthless, but that was only if you didn't know him. To family he was loyal and fiercely protective.

For all appearances, his family now included Tilly. As Keaton and Tilly drank the scotch Kipling poured them, they gave him the rundown of what happened at Tilly's apartment. When they finished, Kipling didn't say anything but stood and poured his own drink. He didn't speak again until he sat down.

"I don't like it," Kipling said. "Not one bit. You did the right thing, though." He sighed. "I'm not sure what's gotten into the Charleston PD. It's utter bullshit they didn't do more than they did. Though it does sound like Alyssa has a brain in her head, unlike the other so called police officers."

"That's what I told Tilly." Keaton stroked her arm and chucked when she attempted to stifle a yawn. "I think it's time we turned in."

Kipling nodded. "Go get her settled. I'll have your car taken care of."

"Thank you." Keaton stood to his feet, holding Tilly close to him. "Come on," he told her. "Let me show you where the rooms are just in case you've forgotten."

"Tilly," Kipling called out and the couple turned to face him. "It goes without saying, but you're welcome to stay here for as long as you need."

"Thank you," she whispered, and she sounded so fragile, Keaton tugged her closer. He couldn't help think how perfect she felt in his arms.

He'd dropped her overnight bag in the foyer when they came in and Maggie, that woman needed a raise, had already taken it upstairs to the guest room.

Though she'd been yawning in the living room, the walk to the bedrooms seemed to have woken Tilly a bit. Her eyes darted around the hallways, and he wondered how much had changed since she'd last been inside.

"It's so strange being back here," she said. "It all looks so familiar, yet different."

He knew exactly what she was talking about, but he didn't want to think about the past. Too much wasted time. He wanted to focus on the future because the more time he spent with her, the more he saw Tilly being a part of it.

Once inside the guest room, Keaton pointed. "There's a full bath through that door, and Maggie should have set you out a toothbrush."

Tilly nodded, wrapping her arms around her body. "Where will Elise be staying?"

"She'll be at the opposite end of the hall." At her nod, he added. "Simply because Kipling wouldn't let me stick her in the pool house."

That got a half smile out of her, but it quickly faded. "Is it stupid that I'm not looking forward to seeing her?"

Keaton closed the bedroom door. "No. I'm not overly pleased about her being here either."

JADE

It had been both stupid and dangerous for me to stick around. I don't know why King gave me the job in the first place. It seemed an inordinate amount of effort for little perceived reward.

The policewoman who showed up confirmed my suspicion that the Benedicts didn't have a clue as to what was going on, and I should have left. But I couldn't stop myself from slashing the Benedict guy's tires. I did that just for fun. Then I hid and waited for the show to start.

The satisfaction I'd anticipated seeing Keaton and Tilly scared and confused never came. They spoke for a few minutes when the policewoman came back, but things got even more boring after she left. It wasn't much fun watching Keaton and Tilly wait for the car service to show up. Plus, it was getting late and I'd been up since before dawn.

I slowly backed out of my hiding place, and, with a yawn, turned around. Before I could take a step forward, I was captured and held tightly by two strong arms. A large hand was clamped over my mouth, making it impossible for me to scream.

"I could snap your neck and he'd never know," a familiar voice said roughly in my ear.

Kevan.

I bit his hand, and he let me go with a chuckle. "Asshole," I said, hating myself for the way my cheeks heated at his nearness. The guy was too damn good looking for his own good.

"Not my problem you weren't paying attention."

He was right, and I didn't have anything to say in response to his statement so I changed the subject. "What are you doing here?"

"His Majesty wanted me to follow you to make sure everything went according to plan."

I wasn't sure which shocked me more, Kevan's blatant disrespect of King or that King thought I needed a babysitter. "You better make sure he doesn't hear you call him that."

He shrugged, seemingly unconcerned. It was an attitude I'd never seen anyone have when it came to King. Even if you didn't fear him, you still deferred to him. Or at least that's what people did in my experience.

"Why did he feel it necessary for you to follow me?" I asked instead of digging further into the hows and whys of the way he spoke about King. After all, it was his funeral.

"Why does he do anything?" Kevan asked. "I don't know. He asked me to follow you, and I did. Seemed liked the smartest thing to do."

And that was the most intelligent thing he'd said thus far. "Do you have a part in the Benedict plan?" I asked.

"Not that I know of," he replied. "Not beyond following you when told."

I had started on my way back to the warehouse, my name for the building I lived in. When I was younger, I used to call it home, but as I grew older, I learned it was only one of many residential properties King owned, and it wasn't even his main residence. I didn't have a home, but King did. A real one, where he lived with his real family, a wife and a daughter I'd never met.

I'd been devastated the day I learned about them, but that was years ago. I'd long since learned I was in this life alone.

"Are you going back to the warehouse with me?" I asked Kevan. It wouldn't be unheard of; Kevan had a room there, though he seldom used it.

"No," he said. "I have other business to take care of."

"Other business of King's?" I wasn't sure why the question popped into my head, but once it did, it just flew out of my mouth.

"What other kind is there?" he asked, and before I could answer, he winked. "See you around."

As I stood watching him walk away in the opposite direction I was headed, I realized that the past few minutes had been the longest conversation Kevan and I had ever had. I couldn't shake the feeling there was more to the discussion than what had been spoken.

CHAPTER 12

The next morning as Keaton turned the final corner of his morning run, his heart sank. He dropped his speed from a jog to a walk and then from a walk to a stroll, cursing under his breath the entire time.

There was only one reason for a black limo to be parked in his driveway.

Elise had arrived early.

He considered turning around and heading back out, but before he could get his feet to move, the front door opened and Elise stepped out. She spotted him almost immediately, of course. She lifted her arm in a wave.

Damn it. No way could he pretend he didn't see her, not with her eyes locked on his the way they were. With a sigh, he continued walking up the drive. By the time he made it to where she was, her father, Howard, had joined her.

"Keaton," her father said with a nod and a handshake. "Congratulations on your graduation."

"Thank you, sir. Nice to see you again."

Mr. Germain nodded toward his daughter. "Look after my girl this summer."

"We all will, sir." Keaton didn't think he'd imagined the look of spite Elise gave her dad before her features settled once more into nothing.

"Hello, Keaton," Elise said and he turned to her.

She was so perfectly good-looking, she looked fake. From her perfectly styled blonde hair, to her perfect body, hid by her perfectly tailored sundress. Her perfection did nothing for him.

"Hello, Elise. You look well."

Elise wrinkled her nose. "You can welcome me proper after you shower."

Keaton shrugged. He didn't want to touch her anyway. "Have you had breakfast yet?" he asked. "I was going to get a shower and then eat a quick bite."

"Yes," Mr. Germain said. "We ate before we headed out."

"I'll sit with you while you eat," Elise said to him.

"No need for you to do that," Keaton said. "I'm sure you need to unpack and get settled in."

"It can wait," she said in a perfectly sweet voice that make him feel sick. "I'd much rather hear what you've been up to since we last saw each other."

Of course she would.

"I'll put some stuff away while you shower," she said like it was the most brilliant idea ever.

"I have to go," Mr. Germain said. He gave Keaton a slap on the shoulder before turning to his daughter and pointing at her. "Be good."

"Aren't I always?"

"I'm not answering that."

Keaton stood in front of the house with her while she watched her father get into the limo and leave the property. Elise turned to him as soon as the car disappeared. All traces of the sugary sweet Daddy's girl was gone. The woman before him was cold and calculating.

"I heard about what happened at that club," Elise said. "You should know better than to lower your standards like that. And you sure as hell need to be more discrete."

Any reply he gave would do nothing but escalate the situation. With that in mind, he did the only other thing possible. He turned and walked away to take a shower.

"Come in," Tilly said at the knock on the guest bedroom door. She'd only been up for short time, but had already showered and dressed, and had been contemplating trying to find some breakfast.

Keaton opened the door and stepped inside. "Hey there." His hair was damp from his own shower, and though he was smiling, Tilly sensed something lurking behind his eyes.

"Everything okay?" she asked. "I heard a bit of commotion earlier."

Keaton sighed. "Elise arrived early."

Tilly could only nod and try to come to terms with the fact that she'd soon be face-to-face with her once upon a time best friend. "How is she?" she managed to ask.

"I suppose by anyone's standards she's doing well," Keaton said. "She looked okay, but she's so pale, she probably keeps the sun block industry in business single-handedly. Her eyes are blue. I don't remember that, must be contacts."

"She always was beautiful."

"She does nothing for me."

Tilly schooled her features and tried to keep her expression neutral as they walked into the dining room.

"Oh my god, Tilly!"

Tilly winced at Elise's shrill welcome.

Keaton pulled out a chair at the opposite end of the table and Tilly sat, pleased when he took the seat at her side.

He glared at the blonde. "Damn, Elise. Take it down a few notches."

The fake smile Elise had been wearing faltered a bit, and she opened her mouth to reply.

"Good morning, everyone." Kipling strolled into the dining, effectively shutting down Elise. He sat down and poured a cup of coffee. "Keaton, your car's in the driveway, and Tilly, your apartment will be cleaned by noon."

The long reaching, all powerful arm of the Benedicts never failed to amaze her. Though before that power had been used against her family. It was an odd comfort to be on the safe side.

And no matter what Keaton or Kipling said, she was going to pay them back for the cleaning service.

"Thank you," Tilly said. "I guess I can go back later today."

Kipling looked to Keaton, who only answered with, "The hell you will." She tried to say something, but he cut her off. "We don't know who it was or if they'll come back. You're staying here."

"You can't force her, you know," Elise said.

"We aren't forcing anyone to do anything," Kipling said. "Keaton, calm down. Tilly, until we have additional information, I do think it would be best for you to remain here."

"I don't want to be an imposition." She looked at Elise. "You already have one house guest."

"Maggie is thrilled to have a house full again. Trust me,

if you leave now, she'll mope for days." Kipling gave her a rare smile. "Don't break her heart, Tilly."

He was being overly dramatic, which really wasn't like the Kipling she remembered, but it was a nice change to Keaton's overprotectiveness. Though, that was nice, too. It felt good to be wanted. She knew Keaton wanted her to stay, but she wasn't sure she'd have considered it if Kipling didn't feel the same way.

Keaton pushed back from the table. "I need to take care of a few things. Walk with me outside, Tilly?"

"Sure." She stood and followed him out, not missing the heated scorn of Elise's gaze on her back.

He waited until they were out of earshot before talking. "I'll be back in about an hour and then I want to look into the key you mentioned. Please tell me you'll still be here when I get back."

She had brought the key up in passing the night before but not in any detail. "I promise I won't go anywhere. I'll stay here with Elise and Kipling."

"Just Elise. Kipling's probably going into the office."

Ugh. Suddenly she remembered one of the reasons why she wanted to leave. "I don't suppose there's anything you can do to keep Elise in her room while you're gone, is there?"

"Not that won't get me arrested."

"Don't even joke. I've had enough of police officers to last me for just about forever."

"I'll be back as soon as I can." He gave her a quick kiss and was off.

She didn't want to go back into the dining room, but she refused to let Elise get the best of her. So instead of hiding out in the guest room, she squared her shoulders and went to face the woman who used to be her best friend.

It was quiet when she made it into the dining room, but she remembered Keaton saying that Kipling was Elise's least favorite brother. Unfortunately, Kipling appeared to finishing his breakfast, and she knew he'd soon be on his way to the office. Her fear was confirmed when he stood right as she sat down.

Elise, strangely, didn't say a word until he'd pulled out of the driveway. When she turned to face Tilly, gone was the debutant and in her place was a calculating shrew.

"Pretty ballsy move you made," Elise said. "Coming back here in an attempt to get back in the good graces of the Benedict brothers and get your claws into Keaton at the same time."

Even though Tilly had half expected the change in demeanor, it still came as a shock. That was the only explanation she could come up with as to why she replied the way she did. "Is that what I'm doing? Funny. I thought you were the one with aspirations of being Mrs. Keaton Benedict. Or is there another reason why you just happened to be interning in Charleston?"

"I don't have aspirations of any sort because I don't need them. A union between my family and the Benedicts has been in the works since before you were born."

Tilly ate a bite of egg to keep from saying anything.

"I can't say I blame you for not wanting to stay here, you know, earlier when Kipling was talking about it?" Elise asked, changing the subject. "I certainly wouldn't want to hang out with people who were only putting up with me out of respect for my mother."

"What?" Tilly asked.

"Everyone loved your mother, Tilly. Anne was the sweetest and dearest woman anyone ever met. But your dad was a rat. You know he was running around on your mom."

Tilly couldn't believe the lies spewing from Elise's mouth. How was it lightning hadn't struck her dead yet? "He did not." It was paltry, but they were the only words she could manage to get out at the moment.

"Please. Grow up. Everyone knew about it. Why do you think you and Anne spent so much time over here?" Elise asked.

Because before the scandal that ruined her family, her mother and Keaton's mother had been best friends. They were always doing things together. Shopping, volunteering, hosting parties.

"Oh my god," Elise said. "You really didn't know?"

She sounded surprised, but Tilly had a feeling she'd been planning what to say since the second she heard Tilly would be hanging around.

"That's because it's completely made up." It had to be, her father had been one of the kindest men she'd even known. He'd adored his wife.

Elise stood with a look of pity that made Tilly's stomach turn. She had to be lying. She had to be.

"I guess for some people, reality is just too hard to live with. That's okay, you can live in your make believe land." Elise stood and smoothed her skirt. "I'm going to go shopping. Alone."

Tilly tried not to snort as her ex-best friend walked away. Did Elise actually think Tilly would ask if she could go along? Seriously?

AFTER BREAKFAST, Tilly stayed in the guest room until she heard Elise leave. She strolled though the hallways, remembering snatches of her childhood she hadn't thought of in ages. Benedict House was so familiar and yet, oddly different at the same time.

Eventually, she found herself in the kitchen where Maggie was preparing lunch. Tilly remembered her from years past. "Can I help?"

Maggie turned with her hand over her heart. "Tilly. Lord, it does these old bones good to see you in my kitchen again." She held out her arms. "Come here."

Tilly walked into her embrace and held back tears as Maggie whispered how much she'd missed her. And even though she'd known Elise had lied about no one wanting her, it felt good to have that assumption proven wrong. Being held by Maggie wasn't the exact same as being held by her mother, but it was the closest she'd be able to find on earth.

"I know you've had some trouble the last few days," Maggie said. "But it's so good to see you again. This place was never the same without you and your mama."

"It's so good to see you."

Maggie took a step back and looked Tilly up and down. "Look at you. Beautiful."

Tilly's cheeks heated. "Maggie."

"I mean it, and you're just as beautiful on the inside. Unlike some people." Maggie shook her head. "That Germain girl is nothing but bad news and trouble, mark my word. Mrs. Helen would never stand for Mr. Keaton to marry such a ball of fluff."

"Keaton told me he had no intention of marrying Elise."

"Good, he needs someone like you."

Tilly shook her head. "Don't even think about going there. I'm not sure I even like him very much."

Maggie gave her a *do-you-think-I'm-stupid* look.

"Doesn't matter how many times you tell yourself that lie, you'll never believe it." She turned back to the stove. "Now enough of that jabbering, you said you wanted to help?"

"Yes, ma'am."

"How about you make a nice salad for lunch? All three of my boys will be here, and Mr. Knox likes salads. Mr. Kipling needs more greens in his diet. Mr. Knox says it's lack of nutrients that makes his brother so ornery. I told him what Mr. Kipling needed was to get laid."

"Maggie!" Tilly laughed. "I can't believe you said that."

"Why? Because old people don't know about getting laid? Please, how the hell do you think you got here?"

Being in the Benedict's kitchen was the closest to feeling as if she was at home than anything she'd experienced in years. She stayed with Maggie, making lunch, talking, and laughing until she heard Keaton return.

Maggie snorted at the way she dropped her knife when the side door of the house opened. "Not even sure you like him?"

CHAPTER 13

"There you are," Keaton said, pushing the door of his room open at her knock. "I was getting ready to come hunt you down."

"I was in the kitchen helping Maggie with lunch."

He dragged her into the room and closed the door behind them. "I bet she loved that."

"Yes, she did."

He took her hand and tugged her to sit beside him on the small loveseat at the end of bed. "What else did you talk about?"

She picked at imaginary lint on his shirt. "Oh, you know, this and that."

"This and that?"

"Yes," she said, knowing he wanted her to admit they talked about him but wanting to tease him. "Did you know she has seven grandchildren?"

"I did."

"And she still calls you and your brothers *her boys?*"

"Because Maggie's as much a Benedict as we are."

Tilly took a step back as her eyes grew wet. "It's been so long."

"What's been so long?"

"Since there's been anyone other than me. I'm so used to doing it all on my own, it's hard to believe all this." She waved her hand to indicate the room. "All of you and how you take care of each other."

"You better get used to it because I'm not going anywhere and I'm not letting you go." As if to prove his point, he took a step forward. "Well, that's pretty," he said in a whisper.

"What?"

He lightly brushed her bottom lip with his finger. "I believe that's the first real smile I've seen on you since the last time you were here."

Back before her entire life tuned upside down. She refused to walk down that path. It was time to stop living in the past. "I was thinking how nice it was not be alone anymore."

"Never again, Tilly."

She bit the fleshy part of his thumb, surprising herself with her aggressiveness. "Promise."

He sucked in a breath and gave a low moan, but didn't answer. Instead, he leaned close and she followed until his lips brushed over hers. Softly. Almost a tease. In fact, it would have been a tease if they hadn't touched hers again. Stronger though, as if he'd been testing her, making sure she wasn't going to pull away.

She had no plans to do anything of the sort.

"I can't believe you're here," he whispered against her lips. "Before you came back I never knew I could be so happy."

"I'm happy, too." As soon as she spoke the words, it felt

as if an invisible weight had been removed from her shoulders.

"Good." He kept his gaze locked on hers. "Get used to it."

Yes, she definitely could, she decided, trying to remember the last time she felt anything remotely similar. Maybe before her mom died? It didn't make sense for her to feel it now. After all, two people she knew had been murdered, her apartment was a wreck, and though she was staying with Keaton, so was her crazy ex-best friend.

But none of that took away from her happiness.

"I'll try," she promised and lifted her head for another kiss when the silence was broken by someone screaming for Keaton.

"Was that Maggie?" Tilly asked.

Keaton pulled away, his eyebrows knit together in concentration. "Maybe, but I've never heard her sound like that."

They hurried to the stairs.

"I don't think it could be Elise," Tilly said. "She left to go shopping right after you left."

From the top of the staircase, they could see the open front door, but the angle didn't allow them to see anything else.

"Maggie?" Keaton jogged down the stairs and Tilly followed.

"In the foyer," Maggie called.

They rounded the bottom of the massive staircase, and the expanse of the foyer came into view. Maggie was trying to ease someone onto a cushioned bench and started talking as soon as she saw Keaton.

"I was outside and heard a car door slam," Maggie said, letting Keaton take whoever it was from her. "Didn't think anything of it until I heard this moaning sound and this lady here was trying to make her way up the drive. Fell before I got to her and passed right out."

"Let's get her somewhere more comfortable. Maggie, call 911 and get me some towels." Keaton had the woman in his arms and carried her into the living room where he laid her gently on a couch. It wasn't until he stepped back that Tilly could see her.

Pale red hair covered her face, but it was the massive amount of blood and a swollen eye that obscured her identity. At the moment, she wasn't moving. Keaton fell to his knees and grabbed her wrist. "She has a pulse. I know head wounds bleed a lot but this is horrible. I think most of it is from her nose."

Maggie reappeared clutching a phone in one hand and a towel in the other. Keaton took it. "I think the bleeding stopped." He pulled the woman's hair away from her face, and one eye fluttered open twice before closing again.

"Oh my god," Tilly said, dropping to her knees beside him. "It's Bea!"

"Bea?"

"Bea Jacobs. She's an attorney who helped Mama once. You know Brent Taylor?"

Keaton nodded. Anyone with ties to South Carolina knew who Brent Taylor was.

"This is Bea, his half sister."

"Bea," Tilly spoke softly. "It's me, Tilly Brock, and this is Keaton Benedict. Can you open your eyes again for me?"

The eye that wasn't swollen shut opened a tiny bit. "Benedict?" Bea asked in a whisper.

"Yes, you're at Benedict House." Tilly glanced at Keaton and he nodded for her to go on. "We've called for help. They'll be here soon."

Bea licked her lips and seemed to be struggling to talk.

"Shhh. Don't move, you might start bleeding again." Tilly stroked her forehead, but Bea shook her head. Realizing it was pointless, Tilly finally gave in. "Tell me."

Bea took a deep shuddering breath."Knox."

The word was spoke so softly, Tilly was certain she'd heard wrong. "What?"

"Knox." Bea spoke it stronger this time and there was no doubt as to what she said.

"Knox is my brother," Keaton said. "I'm Keaton. The youngest."

Bea shook her head. "Call Knox…"

Beside her, Keaton sucked in a breath.

"What?" Tilly asked. "Bea?"

But speaking those few words had completely wiped Bea out. Her eyes were closed, and though she was breathing and her pulse was steady, neither Tilly or Keaton could rouse her again.

In the distance, the wailing of sirens gradually became louder and louder. Keaton stood and reached in his pocket for his phone. He kept his eyes on Bea as he dialed.

"We have a situation," he said to whoever answered. "Get to the hospital and meet me at the emergency entrance. Now."

CHAPTER 14

To say the hospital waiting room was tense would be an understatement. It would be like calling the sun hot or the ocean wet. Tilly sat beside Keaton and they both watched as Knox paced the floor. Every so often, he'd move from his path in front of the window and make a detour to the clerk's desk to ask if there was any news even though he'd been told repeatedly he would be alerted as soon as there was an update.

The one thing Knox hadn't done was talk to his younger brother. When they'd arrived at the hospital behind the ambulance, Knox was already inside, pacing.

Tilly looked at the large clock on the wall. Maybe she should go get some water for Knox.

Before she could get the words out to ask if he wanted any, the waiting room door opened and Kipling walked in. He glanced at Keaton and Tilly but focused his attention on Knox.

"Want to tell me why Bea Jacobs showed up at Benedict House after being beaten to a bloody pulp?" Kipling asked.

"Not now," Knox said, speaking for the first time.

"Honest to god," Kipling continued. "Between you and Keaton, I don't know what the hell is going on with this family."

Knox grabbed his brother by the collar. "I said, not fucking now."

Tilly had no doubt Kipling could pound Knox into the ground. Kipling's eyes flashed and for a minute, she feared he might take a swing. She breathed a sigh of relief when instead, he calmly said, "Get your hands off of me."

Wisely, Knox listened. Kipling straightened his collar and stepped away. "I'm going to give you a pass this time since you're obviously upset and not thinking, but put your hands on me again, and I'm kicking your ass."

"Did I come at a bad time?"

All eyes moved to the door where Alyssa and her partner stood.

"Would you leave if I said yes?" Kipling asked.

"I wish," Alyssa said. "We're here about Bea Jacobs. Do you know anything about her assault or how she made her way your house?"

"No. I didn't know anything had happened until Keaton left me a voicemail," Kipling said.

The officer looked over at Keaton and raised an eyebrow. "Of course. Mr. Benedict. Ms. Brock."

Tilly felt Keaton tense beside her. "When we saw her, she was already hurt and in our house," he said.

"You didn't see anything?"

"No, our housekeeper found her outside."

"Thank you," Alyssa's partner said. "We'll go talk to her and then come back here to see if Bea's awake."

Not long after they left, a door at the side of the room opened and a woman wearing green scrubs stepped into the waiting room.

"Knox Benedict?" she asked, looking at the brothers.

"That's me," Knox said.

"Come with me."

There were numerous unasked questions on Knox's expression, but instead of voicing them, he nodded and followed her out of the waiting room.

As soon as he left, Kipling turned to Keaton. "Do you know what's going on?"

"I have no idea."

Kipling ran his hand through his hair. "They didn't say how Bea was. I hope she's okay."

Though it seemed longer, it had only been about fifteen minutes when Knox came back to the room. He looked even worse than before.

The two brothers stood. Tilly held her breath, bracing herself for the worst.

"How is she? Is everything okay?" Kipling was the first to speak.

Knox winced. "*Okay* is a relative term. As for how she is, she's alive."

Keaton reached out to touch his shoulder, but Knox twisted away.

An uncomfortable silence fell across the room. Tilly wanted to disappear into the air. She felt there was something else. Something Knox knew but couldn't say or didn't want to say in front of her. Whatever was going on between the brothers was private, leaving her feeling odd and out of place. She thought about returning to the house but didn't want to draw attention to herself.

Knox sighed. "I'm staying here until she gets out; you guys might as well go home. No need for you to stay."

No one left right away. About a half hour later, the two police officers showed up again. Knox mumbled that they wouldn't learn anything from Bea. She'd told him she was attacked from behind.

But when they returned to the waiting room sometime later, Alyssa pulled her and Keaton aside.

"Bea wasn't able to tell us much," Alyssa said. "Just that he made threats against the Benedicts and those close to them."

Tilly froze in place, and immediately, Keaton put his arm around her.

"You need to find this guy and find him *now*," Keaton ground out.

"We're working as hard as we can."

"Work harder."

When the police left, Keaton looked at Tilly and raised his eyebrow. She nodded, ready to leave. Keaton spoke with his brothers for a few minutes, then took her hand. She held her breath as they approached the car. Keaton looked everything over and found nothing. Apparently, the attack on Bea was all their unknown assailant had planned for the day.

KEATON HAD one goal the next morning when Tilly left to visit several banks to see if they were connected to the key —to stay away from Elise. He called Knox, who said Bea was doing better physically but still wasn't saying much. He did research on the charity he wanted to set up and finally felt a sense of relief when he realized Tilly should be back in within the hour.

He should take her out for lunch so they wouldn't have to worry about Elise being an unwelcome third party. He left Kipling's home office where he'd been working and jogged up the stairs to his room, freezing completely when he found Elise sitting on his bed.

"Get out," he said through clenched teeth. "I don't want you in here."

Elise had a sly grin. "You think this is about what *you* want? You poor misguided fool."

"Out. Now."

"I don't think it's wise for you to kick me out without hearing my deal first."

"You must have me confused with Kipling. I'm not the dealmaker in the family."

She still wore that damn grin. Like no matter what he said, she somehow knew this conversation was going to go the way she wanted. "This is nice." She patted the bed. "But I think I'd like a firmer mattress. I find it much more conducive to sex."

He felt his blood begin to boil. She had some nerve. "Your opinion on my choice of mattress is irrelevant. I wouldn't fuck you if we were the last two humans on earth and needed to repopulate the planet."

"So stubborn. Let me be more frank. Not only will you fuck me, you're going to marry me because I have some rather damning information about your dad." He started to protest, but she held up her hand. "Not only that, but if you refuse, I can work it to where it appears as if all the Benedict brothers knew about it. Benedict Industries will be ruined."

Was she serious? "I don't believe you."

She appeared entirely too joyful for his taste. "The Benedict men are known for being players. It's part of your nature, and I understand. That's why I haven't put a stop to you and Tilly. But rest assured, it's coming."

He rolled his eyes. "Can we get on with it, I'm taking Tilly out to lunch."

He didn't imagine the flash of ire in her expression before she continued. "It's not your fault women spread their legs for Benedict cock, and I don't blame you for giving it to them. After all, it's in your genes. A lesson I believe your mom learned early."

He did his best to hide his grimace. He'd always suspected his father cheated on his mom, but to have it so well known that Elise knew about it, was embarrassing.

"Of course, your father took the necessary precautions. After all, he didn't want to be bothered with bastard children." There was no denying it now, Elsie was positively elated to be sharing this story with him. "But, as you're aware, the only effective way to ensure no one gets pregnant is to not have sex. I think we both know that celibacy is not an option for Benedict men."

He had a fairly good idea where she was headed, but surely she knew it'd take more than an illegitimate child in his family's past for him to marry her.

"As was bound to happen, one of your father's mistresses got pregnant. When this happened previously, your father paid handsomely for the woman to take care of it." Elise shook her head. "But this one decided, against your father's wishes, to keep the child. But fearing for her life, as well as that of her daughter's, she vanished. You have to give it to her. She remained hidden for five years."

Keaton's heart pounded and sweat ran down his back. He had a sister? Granted, she would be a half sister, but still...he'd always wanted a sister.

"I'm not exactly sure what happened when the child turned five. If I had to guess, I'd say the ex-mistress contacted your dad, perhaps believing he'd become enamored with the idea of a daughter after having three boys. Unfortunately, that wasn't the case. There was an incident at the shelter they were staying at and both mother and daughter were killed. Of course, there was no evidence your father was involved."

The fact she stood there so calmly only served to prove how cunning she was. "I don't believe you."

Elise shrugged. "Funny thing about the truth. It doesn't matter what you think. It just is. Nothing you do can change that."

"You expect me to believe my father not only had a bastard child, but that he somehow arranged for them both to be killed?" It was beyond ridiculous. "And you think I'm going to marry you because of this made up shit? Get out of my room."

She laughed. Fucking laughed. "I have proof. Of course, all I have with me are photos and copies. I'm not stupid enough to bring you the originals. But I do have them, along with emails and bank statements. I can make it look like the three of you were in on it with your father and you've been covering it up all these years. Contrary to what you think, I learned a lot at college."

He told himself not to panic. He would look over her "proof" and make a plan then. He'd show it to Kipling. Normally, he'd show it to Knox, but with Bea in the hospital, he was out of commission for the moment.

"Show me," he told Elise.

"So impatient. You'll get it when I'm ready. Right now, I want you to think about how we're going to announce our engagement. And, just so you know, there will be no discussing things with either Knox or Kipling. If I find out they know, the deal is off, and I'll fucking crush Benedict Industries." She smirked at him and ran a perfectly manicured nail down his chest. "Now, why don't you come to my room, and I'll grab my phone so I can prove everything."

He was going to be sick. Fortunately, Elise didn't say anything more. She gracefully rose to her feet and walked out the door. As the sound of her heels grew faint, he realized how much he underestimated her.

TILLY SMILED at sight of Keaton waiting for her she pulled into the driveway. She'd borrowed one of the many cars in the garage earlier and taken the mystery key with her to a few banks. Unfortunately, none of them could help, but seeing Keaton made her feel better. Until she got closer and saw his frown and the worry line etched in his face.

"Is it Bea?" She paused. "Is she worse?"

"No." Keaton looked around like he was expecting someone to be watching or listening. It freaked her out. He nodded to the car. "Can I drive?"

"Sure." She tossed him the keys and walked around to get in on the passenger side.

He didn't say anything, and though she wanted to ask him what was wrong, the tense set of his jaw kept her silent. Whatever it turned out to be was going to be bad.

JADE

Once upon a time, I believed every word King said. I was so starved for acceptance and love, I'd do anything he asked without question. After all, King was my god and you didn't question your god.

But little by little, I became aware he was all too human and started questioning him, if only in my head.

I didn't like the answers I found.

All my life, or as far back as I could remember, I'd been taught the Benedict family was evil, a blight on humanity, and needed to be taken down. But standing in the shadows of their garden, watching Keaton and Tilly drive away, they didn't look evil.

I knew that evil had many faces and a lot of them were pleasant, but I couldn't stop thinking that something wasn't adding up. How could the couple in front of me be evil when all they wanted to do was help people?

Nothing about them or this place appeared bad. On the contrary, it felt warm and inviting. Half of me wanted nothing more than to be a part of it. The other half wanted to walk up the long stone drive and be welcomed inside. The only thing was, if they were warm and inviting and good, then everything I'd ever been told was a lie. I wasn't ready to believe that just yet.

CHAPTER 15

It wasn't until they were out of the city and on the highway that Keaton spoke.

"Elise is blackmailing me," he said.

"What?" Surely, she'd heard incorrectly. "*Elise?*"

"It's crazy as hell, but she says she has proof Dad fathered an illegitimate daughter and then had her and her mother killed."

"That's ridiculous."

"That was my first thought, but she had emails and bank statements. Told me to think about it." He spoke the words with disgust.

"What did Knox and Kipling say?"

He shook his head. "She says I can't tell them or else she'll set us all up."

"She's bat shit crazy."

"I know. But the thing is, it's so crazy, I can't see her making it up."

"Why would she blackmail you, though? Doesn't her family have money? I mean, they're as rich as you guys, right?"

"It's not money she wants," he said quietly.

It took her a few seconds to register what he said and what it meant. "Oh, god," she said as understanding dawned.

"Yeah." He clenched his jaw for a second and then took a deep breath. "Exactly."

"What are you going to do?"

"That's what I wanted to talk to you about. I wanted to get your opinion. Obviously, I'm not doing anything until I see this so called 'proof' she has."

"That might be all it takes. For you to call her bluff."

"If only it would be that easy."

Tilly had a sinking suspicion that he was right. "And if it turns out it looks legit?"

"I don't know, but I'm sure as hell not marrying her."

"Of course not." She put a hand on his thigh and felt the tension leave his body at her touch. "Even if it turns out she's right, it wasn't anything you or your brothers did. How could she destroy Benedict Industries?"

Keaton kept his focus on the road. "She threatened to set us up if I told Knox or Kip, I have to assume she has a way."

Deep down, she knew he was right. "I hate her so much.Why did she pick now to do her internship?"

"A question I've been asking myself for days." He sighed. "I can't stand the thought of going back to the house and seeing her smug smile."

"Then let's don't," she said. "I'm sure we can find a hotel with a room somewhere."

He glanced at her. "A room? As in one?"

She inched her fingers up his thigh and smiled at his sharp intake of breath. "Yes. With one bed."

. . .

IT WASN'T anything for a Benedict to be seen getting a hotel room for one night. Keaton had done it a time or two himself, and he had little doubt he could walk into any hotel in Charleston and procure a room. But this was different. More than one of his dates had been photographed leaving a hotel after a night with him, and he didn't want that for Tilly. She wasn't a one night stand he didn't want in his home.

He took an exit off the highway. "Folly Beach work for you?"

She gave a soft chuckle that made him smile.

"I'll take that as a yes," he replied.

He pulled into the parking lot of an upscale hotel. "Do you want to stay in the car while I check us in or come with me?"

"No need for both of us to go," she said. "I'll stay here."

It only took him a few minutes to secure a room, and after he parked the car, he led her to their suite. He hated how awkward he felt. Normally when he met a woman at a hotel, he was full of confidence. But not so with Tilly. She kept him on his feet.

Much like the current situation they were in. "Did we really just get a hotel room without having luggage, a change of clothes, or anything?" he asked.

She moved to stand in front of him. Her fingers brushed up and down his arm, and he bit his tongue to keep from moaning at her touch.

"I was under the impression clothes wouldn't be necessary," she said.

"I don't want you to feel like we have to do anything." Maybe she'd only been teasing in the car. "We can just talk."

"That's good to know." She kept her eyes on him, pulled

his head down and whispered, "Take me to bed, Keaton, and if that's not clear enough, maybe this will be. Fuck me. Now." Before he could say anything, her lips were on his and leaving no doubt that talking was the last thing she wanted. And judging from the way she spoke and kissed him, anything soft and gentle was off the table as well.

Fine by him. "If you insist."

She gasped as he grabbed her wrists and held them above her head. He shifted his weight so she could feel his hard length.

He was hanging on by a thread and needed her to understand before they moved forward. "I can't be slow or gentle right now," he said. "Tell me now if that's not okay or not what you want, and I'll go take a cold shower or run five miles."

He half expected her to tell him to stop, but she surprised him by biting his earlobe. "Take me however you need. I'm yours."

He pulled back to see the truth of her words reflected in her eyes.

He wasn't sure what he'd ever done to deserve Tilly. She was accepting of him, even at his most unlovable, and she was quickly becoming vital to him. The realization of just how necessary shook him to his core. It was more than the need to have her physically or even the need to simply have her in his life. He needed her to be safe and at that moment, he knew he'd give up his own life to keep her that way.

Keeping her hands immobilized in his grip, he took her lips in a brutal kiss, tasting her, imprinting everything about her to his memory. She whimpered deep in her throat and lifted her right leg and hooked it around his waist, drawing him closer, even as he feared he should pull back.

Unable to stop himself, he let go of her wrists and

yanked her shirt over her head. She looked at him with lust-filled eyes.

"You like it when I'm rough." It wasn't a question and she didn't answer.

His hands dropped to the waistband of her jeans, and he hurriedly unbuttoned them. He growled as she repeated the action on him. He pushed the denim below her hips, leaving only a scrap of silk between him and what he wanted.

He shoved the silk aside and pushed two fingers inside her. "Damn, Tilly. You're soaked." He pumped in and out several times, removing his hand completely when her body shook with an impeding release. "Not yet. I want to feel you shatter around me."

"Now."

He hadn't thought he could get any harder but that one word proved him wrong. He bent down, taking her jeans with him, but stood without removing his. She raised an eyebrow at him.

"I'm not even going to bother taking my jeans or your underwear off," he said. "I'm going to take you just like this: dirty, raw, and hard."

Her only reply was a shaky, "Yes," that ended with a sharp intake of breath.

That was the only word he needed. "Turn around and face the wall."

She whimpered but moved into position, bending slightly at the waist to give him better access. He stroked himself wondering if she had any idea how damn sexy she was.

True to his word, he only unzipped his jeans enough to remove his cock, and she let out a moan when he pressed it against the silk on her backside.

"Feel how hard I am?" he asked, slipping on a condom. "You do this to me. Only you."

But it seemed Tilly was beyond talking. She nodded. He pushed the tiny scrap of material between her legs out of the way and with one hard thrust, buried himself inside her.

Her head fell back, and she clenched around him as her climax overtook her.

"Damn, Tilly," he said in a half growl.

He started a rough rhythm, but based on her gasps of pleasure, she didn't mind. Everything about her felt so good. He'd never been with anyone who could both capture his mind and make his body rise. He leaned over her back and in low whispers, told her how beautiful she was, how sexy, and that she was made for him. Feeling her second release approach in time with his own, though, he knew the truth. They were made for each other.

THE NEXT MORNING, Tilly woke relaxed and more rested than she'd felt in ages. Judging by the sunlight streaming in through the small crack in the window, it was relatively early. She looked over Keaton's shoulder and saw it was just after seven.

Odd that she'd wake up so soon, she thought with a smile. After everything they'd done together the day before, she'd expected to sleep until at least ten. Keaton still snored softly. She pushed up on her elbow and placed a soft kiss on his forehead. A flash of light on the nightstand caught her eye.

Someone was calling him. Her heart pounded at the sight of the name. Derrick, the Benedict's lawyer.

"Keaton." She shook his shoulder.

He didn't budge.

"Keaton. Wake up." She shook him harder. "Derrick's trying to get in touch with you."

"What?" He was fully awake now, looking around.

"Your phone just rang. It was him."

He grabbed the phone. "I have a voicemail," he said and held it up to his ear. After listening, he immediately made a call.

"Derrick. It's Keaton." He was quiet as the lawyer spoke, but his face turned an unhealthy pale color, and she scooted closer. He hung up without saying anything.

"Keaton?" she asked, her concern growing with every second that passed.

He didn't look at her. "The police are looking for Kipling."

"Has he been threatened?"

"No, the other blonde twin has been murdered. They think he did it."

CHAPTER 16

Keaton's phone rang almost immediately after he ended the call with his lawyer. "It's Kipling." Tilly appeared to still be processing his previous statement. He answered on speaker. "Where are you?"

"I'm on my way home, and I have all these calls from Derrick? I just tried to call him and got his voicemail instead." He laughed. "You aren't at the police station, are you? I thought for a minute maybe you'd been arrested."

Keaton didn't laugh. He felt numb. Kipling didn't know.

"Keaton?" Kipling said, worrying coloring his tone. "You haven't been arrested, have you?"

"No. But listen to me. The police are looking for you. Tilly and I are meeting Derrick at home. Call him. We'll see you there."

"What? Keaton? Don't hang up."

"The other blonde twin was found murdered last night, and the police want to talk to you. That's all I know. Call Derrick. We'll meet you at home." He disconnected.

Tilly walked over and put her arms around him. "It's

going to be fine. We know he didn't do it, and I'm willing to bet Alyssa knows it, too."

They didn't talk much on the way to Benedict House. Keaton felt himself relax slightly when he saw both Kipling and Derrick's cars in the drive, and no police cruiser in sight. Once inside, they walked to the living room where Derrick sat on a couch and Kipling paced. The oldest Benedict looked up and gave a weak smile at their arrival.

Derrick waved for Tilly and Keaton to sit. "I called that Alyssa woman. She and her partner will be here soon." To Kipling he asked, "You were *where* last night?"

Kipling stopped pacing. "I told you. Maggie's youngest daughter had a ruptured appendix. Her husband is deployed, and the regular sitter was busy. I volunteered to watch their two-year-old son."

Keaton half snorted, half coughed. "You what?"

"He likes ships, and we played boats for three hours until he fell asleep. Maggie wasn't back, so I slept over."

"Oh my god," Keaton said.

Kipling rolled his eyes. "Do me a favor and don't tell anyone."

"I'm afraid we can't make that promise," someone said from the doorway and they all turned to find Alyssa's partner standing at the entranceway to the living room with his arms crossed. By his side stood Alyssa, an unreadable expression on her face.

"Want to tell us what you were doing before you went babysitting?" the policeman said, walking into to living room.

Kipling looked to Derrick, but the lawyer only nodded.

"I went by the office and then walked down the docks." Kipling hesitated only a second before continuing. "I ran into Mandy. We spoke briefly. She propositioned me, and I declined. Right after that, I got the call from Maggie and left."

Alyssa appeared recovered from her stupor at hearing Kipling babysat two-year-olds. "Was Mandy alive when you left her?"

Kipling spun around. "Yes, Officer Adams. Do you really think I killed her and then went to play boats with a baby? Seriously?"

"Just doing my job, Mr. Benedict."

"You're doing it wrong," Kipling countered. "There's a killer running around out there, and instead of finding him, you're harassing me."

"Mandy had traces of semen in her mouth," Alyssa said, and Tilly noticed her partner did not look pleased she'd shared that information.

Kipling didn't miss a beat. "Then you know it wasn't me because I didn't touch her."

Alyssa was silent. For a long second, they stood almost toe to toe each watching the other. But then with a nod to her partner, she broke it with a bombshell. He handed Alyssa a flash-frozen black rose. She held it up to Kipling.

"Have you ever—" she started, but Kipling interrupted.

"Did you get that out of my car?" He looked over to Derrick. "Can they do that without a search warrant?"

Keaton wasn't looking at Derrick, his eyes were on Alyssa and the officer looked stunned. At her partner's cough, she shook herself.

"It didn't come from your car," Alyssa said. "It came from Mandy's body. Kipling Benedict, you have the right to remain silent..."

· · ·

Sitting in the Charleston police station with Derrick and Kipling hours later, Keaton wondered if he'd lost his mind completely.

"I strongly suggest," Derrick said, "that you hire another attorney. I'm not equipped to handle a capital murder case."

"It's not going to be a capital murder case," Kipling said. "I didn't do it."

"As much as I believe you, that's what everybody says." Derrick opened a file he'd placed on the table. "You need someone with expertise beyond what I have. Now, if you want me to act as co-counsel, I can do that. But you need to bring in someone else to be lead."

"Hell, you think I did it."

"You have to admit it's curious that a rare rose in your car made its way to the docks," Keaton said.

"There's more than one rose like that. Keaton was with me when one was delivered to me. " Kipling's jaw tightened. "I found one in my home office days ago. I had it preserved because I'd been getting so many of them, I thought it would be a good idea. It's been in my car ever since. Obviously, someone took it from my car and put it on Mandy's body."

Derrick slammed his folder closed and stood. "I'm not sitting here listening to this. Kipling, I'll be by later with some recommended names for you. In the meantime, keep your mouth shut."

The brothers watched him walk out. "He thinks I did it." Kipling sunk into his chair after Derrick left. "He honestly thinks I did it."

"How's it going securing the bail?" Keaton decided a change in subject was needed. Heck, for all he knew, Alyssa was listening in on their conversation.

"Good, as far as I know. Derrick's admin was working with our accounts people to get everything transferred."

"Sounds promising. Maybe you'll be out of here soon." Keaton paused for a second. "We need to find out who got into your car. Do you think it's the same person who put the rose in your office?"

Kipling didn't have a chance to answer because at that moment the door to the room opened and Alyssa walked in. "Time's up, gentlemen."

Kipling looked at the officer like she was prey to tease. "You know, Officer Adams, if you wanted to spend time with me, you only had to ask. You didn't have to arrest me."

"Mr. Benedict," she said, and her voice was calm and even, though her flushed skin belied her otherwise composed demeanor. "Murder is a very serious charge. It may behoove you to take it seriously."

Kipling tapped the table. "Don't make assumptions, Officer. I'm taking it very seriously, I just happen to know I didn't do it, and that's all I need."

"It would appear you also need an attorney," she said. "Yours told us he's advised you to select new counsel."

"Yes."

"Would you like to answer a few questions now?"

Kipling raised an eyebrow. "Do I look stupid?"

Alyssa crossed her arms. "You're sitting in jail, charged with murder. That leads me to believe you may not be as intelligent as you think yourself to be."

"Rest assured, there is no need to question my intelligence. I know I'm innocent, and regardless of what you think, I'm not so inept I'll answer anything without an attorney present. My staff is transferring the funds needed for bail, and I'll be out of your hair shortly."

"You seem to think you've actually been in my hair.

Trust me, you haven't been. You're part of my job, that's all."

"You know what the best part of your denial is?"

Alyssa smirked. "How it's the truth?"

"How satisfying it's going to be when you finally surrender to me."

"Keep dreaming, Mr. Benedict."

"Is it wrong how much it turns me on when you call me *Mr. Benedict?*"

Keaton kicked him under the table. *Are you insane?* he mouthed to his brother. Kipling shrugged.

"I'm not even going to justify that question with an answer."

Kipling didn't appear to be too upset with her statement. "Follow up and make sure everything's lined up for my bail," he told Keaton. "I really don't want to spend the night here."

Keaton nodded. He'd left Tilly at Benedict House before coming to the station, and wanted to check on her. He thought Elise's internship started today, so she shouldn't be there. Even still, Tilly had been slightly uneasy about the situation. "I'm going by the house, I'll make some phone calls from there."

Though Tilly wasn't thrilled to be alone at Benedict House, her discomfort was underscored by her concern for the brothers. Keaton insisted he was fine, but it was her opinion people weren't fine when their older brother was arrested and charged with murder in front of them.

"Truly," he'd told her. "I'm fine because the only other alternative is to have a breakdown."

She'd told him that she'd stay at the house while he met

with Kipling and Derrick, not just because he'd feel better knowing she was safe, but also because he'd told her Elise started her internship today. The last thing she wanted to deal with was Elise.

After Keaton left, Tilly went to the kitchen. Though Maggie was at the hospital with her daughter, the kitchen had always felt warm and inviting. Just standing in it or walking through could brighten her day.

Unfortunately, that wasn't the case when she ran into her least favorite person. Elise.

"I thought you started your internship today," Tilly said instead of greeting her.

She had to tread lightly. Elise had told Keaton not to say anything to his brothers about the blackmail, but she hadn't said anything about telling Tilly. More than likely it had been an oversight. Odds were, Elise didn't want Keaton telling anyone.

Which meant, at the moment, Tilly had to put on the performance of a lifetime.

"I called and told them I wouldn't be in because of a family emergency." Elise's idea of helping during a family emergency appeared to be doing her nails. "I figured my future brother-in-law being arrested for murder was an emergency, don't you?"

Tilly nodded to Elise's half finished self manicure. "I'm sure Kipling appreciates you taking time to ensure your nails look good."

Anger flashed in Elise's eyes. "You're a real bitch, you know that?"

"Yes."

Elise calmly went back to doing her nails. "I know he fucked you yesterday."

"And this morning."

Tilly had only thought she saw Elise angry before, but the woman in front of her now appeared as if she'd slay her with her eyes alone. *Elise could be very dangerous.* Tilly wasn't sure where the thought came from, but she knew she needed to heed it.

Elise stood so fast, she bumped the table and knocked over an open bottle of nail polish. She didn't turn back to pick it up or clean the mess, but stomped out of the kitchen. Tilly didn't allow herself to feel victorious. She had the sinking feeling that no matter how good it'd felt to say that to Elise, she was going to end up regretting she'd done so.

CHAPTER 17

Later that afternoon, Keaton was working on his proposal for Kipling. Derrick had notified him earlier that bail had been posted and Kipling would be getting out of jail within the next two hours. Tilly was in the Benedict's library looking for information on her mother's key. He didn't know where Elise was, nor did he care. Tilly had filled him in on the conversation she had with Elise when he got back from the station. He thought she handled it as well as she could have, but he agreed it hadn't been a good idea to piss Elise off.

"There you are," the woman in question said from his doorway.

He stopped typing with a big sigh. He had known this was coming. Best to get it over with now.

"I brought copies of the information I told you about," Elise said. "Want to look over everything, ask any questions, and then plan when we should announce our engagement?"

"You sound pretty damn sure of yourself." His stomach

turned at both the thought of looking over the papers and thinking for a minute about being engaged to the woman.

She tossed her hair back over her shoulder, and he wondered if she practiced the move in the mirror. "I have every right to be sure. It's win-win for both of us, Keaton. Eventually, you'll see that."

Doubtful, he thought. If he had all the time in the universe plus an extra million years added on, he would never think marrying Elise was win-win.

He took the papers from her but didn't look at them. Elise remained in place as if waiting for him to do something.

"Don't you have anything to do?" he asked. Seriously, she planned to stand there in his doorway?

"No, not really."

"Well, I do." He stood and closed the door in her face. Like Tilly, he had a feeling that hadn't been the best way to deal with Elise. But it sure did feel good.

His gaze fell on the stack of papers he'd placed on his desk. Hell, he didn't want to look at them. He knew his father had been ruthless in business, but there was a huge difference between being ruthless and having someone murdered in cold blood.

To do so to your own child signified an evil he couldn't comprehend.

He remembered his dad well. The senior Benedict had never been a soft man or one to show emotions easily, but he'd been fiercely protective when it came to his wife and sons.

The questions were, did that protectiveness mean keeping a half sibling from his sons? And if so, how far was he willing to go to ensure they never knew her?

Heart heavy with dread, he reached for the pile and began to read.

Tɪʟʟʏ's ʜᴇᴀᴅ shot up at the sound of the library door closing and breathed a sigh of relief at the sight of Keaton.

"Thank goodness it's you," she said. "I half expected to look up and see Elise."

He didn't smile or say anything, just walked over and sat down beside her. Her heart sank, and her arms went automatically around him. He gave a soft sigh and, maybe it was her imagination, but she thought he relaxed a bit.

"You saw her evidence, didn't you?" That had to be the reason for his broken look. Then it hit her; Keaton's reaction wasn't a result of being blackmailed, it was because something had rocked his very foundation.

She buried her head in his neck. "God, Keaton, I'm so sorry."

He embraced her as a sob ripped through his body. "I had a sister. A little sister."

Tilly knew he wasn't only crying for the sister he never had a chance to meet but also for the man he thought his father was.

He kept his head buried in her hair. "How could he do something like that? Kill his own daughter? She was five! Five! She never even had a chance to live."

"There's no way Elise could have falsified anything?" Tilly asked, because truly, it was the only logical explanation.

He pulled back. "There's nothing I'd like more than for that to be the case. But, I don't see how that's possible. She has phone records showing calls were made from his office phone and bank records clearly showing a pay out. I won't say it's not possible to create all those items, but it wouldn't be easy. Plus, she said she has more to show me."

He started to say something else but stopped. She knew he was holding back. "Tell me."

"I went into the family's online banking records. I've never done that before, I've always left it to Kipling, but they matched." He pulled back and she saw the pain in his eyes. "They matched down to the last penny."

"Don't you think Elise would do anything it took to get her hands on you?" Tilly didn't see a little forgery standing in the way of Elise. Not when it came to Keaton.

"I don't see how she could do this. She'd have to have access to our accounts, and there's no way she does." He took her hand. "I don't know what I'd do without you."

Likewise, she'd hate for him to do it alone. "What are you going to do?"

"I'd really like to sit down with Knox and Kipling to get their take. I mean, they don't even know we had a sister. Who am I to keep her from them?" He took a deep breath. "But I have a feeling I'm going to piss Elise off enough as it is. I really don't need to add more fuel to that fire."

"How do you plan on pissing her off?"

He smiled for the first time since walking into the library. "I'm telling her I'm not going to marry her."

Tilly gave a low whistle. "Piss off is probably too mild to put it."

"If I give into her demands, she wins and my dad wins. After what he did, what do I care about his reputation?"

"But didn't she also say she could set up you and your brothers to make it look as if the three of you were in on it?"

"I think she'd have a hard time pulling that off. Even if she made up everything she has on dad, that's a far cry from setting up three additional people. Especially when there's nothing there."

She trusted him to know what he was doing, knew he realized the risk he was taking. The stakes were high. If he miscalculated and underestimated Elise, he and his brothers could wind up being charged as an accessory to murder.

"I think it's about as good as anything we could come up with," she said. "I hate how risky it is, but I'll do anything I can to support you."

"Thank you. You don't know how much that means."

Tilly had always thought of herself as a kind person. She was easy to get along with and, maybe it was prideful, but she thought most people liked her. Her mother had taught her to try to find the good in everyone.

All and all, when it came down to it, up until that moment, there had never been a person she hated. Oh sure, she disliked her fair share. And then there were those people you would never get along with, no matter how hard you tried. But out and out *hate* someone? Never.

Except for today. Today she could honestly say she hated Elise.

Keaton took her hand, and his eyes lost some of the pain they'd held since he'd walked into the room. "Stay here with me. I can't do this alone."

Joy flooded her soul and she squeezed his hand. "Yes. There's nowhere else I'd rather be."

"I'm not telling Elise anything for the moment," Keaton said. "I'm going to buy some time. See how long I can put her off. But one thing is certain, they'll build a ski resort in hell before I even pretend to be engaged to that woman."

CHAPTER 18

With Kipling back at Benedict House, things started to feel a bit more normal. Or maybe it was better said things felt *almost* normal. Keaton rarely made it through an hour without thinking of the sister he never knew.

A few days after Kipling made bail, Bea was released from the hospital. She still refused to talk to Knox, and interestingly enough, his middle brother stayed at home more. But he was quiet and withdrawn, definitely not his normal self. Not even his *almost* normal self.

Elise had left to spend a long weekend with her grand-mother. Keaton wasn't sure exactly what she was doing with her internship because she never actually seemed to be working. But he wasn't stupid enough to act interested in anything pertaining to her.

After dropping the bombshell about his father, and giving him all the information to back it up, she had been relatively quiet. He tried to see it as a good sign, but more than likely it meant Elise was up to something.

He had yet to tell his brothers about their half sister

knowing it would destroy the image they had of their father. Besides, his brothers had dealt with enough heartache lately; they didn't need the additional burden of the knowledge he had. At least not now.

Later.

He justified keeping it a secret at the moment because if Knox and Kipling didn't know their sister existed, how could Elise possibly pin her murder on them?

"Hey, handsome," Tilly said, coming into his bedroom. "It's Friday night; let's get out of here."

God, he loved this woman. Already, he didn't know what he'd done without her. She grounded him. She understood him. She loved him. She hadn't said the words yet, but he knew.

She told him in the way she looked at him. He felt it in her touch. He tasted it in her kiss. She wrote it on his skin every time she touched him.

Instead of replying to her suggestion, he asked, "Do you get the feeling it's been too quiet lately?"

She crossed the room to where he sat and plopped in his lap. "You mean like it's the quiet before the storm and there's a category five hurricane brewing?"

If there was anything better in the world than a lap full of Tilly, he didn't know what it was. "Yes, exactly like that."

"I've had that feeling since the day I moved in. I approach it like I have every other storm I've been through."

"And how is that?"

"I put up storm shutters, gather those I care for, lock us all in a safe place, and wait it out."

Her eyes sparkled. She was so vibrant and lively. He pushed a lock of hair over her shoulder. "Would you gather me with you?"

"No," she said, shocking him until she added, "You are my safe place."

That surprised him even more and he pulled her closer. "I hope I'm always able to keep you safe. I know I've failed you in the past and I fear it's only a matter of time before I really screw up."

"That's why you're afraid it's been too quiet lately? You think something's going to happen to me?"

He nodded.

"Don't worry about me. I promise I'm a big girl and there's no one and nothing going to come between me and you. I'm not going to let it."

"I know you're strong. I just worry."

"Let's not worry until we have something specific to worry about."

"I have a brother accused of murder, and I'm being blackmailed by a psychopath to marry her. I think we have plenty of specifics to worry about."

"When you put it that way, it makes me want to lock ourselves in your room and never leave." She took hold of his shoulder and pulled him toward her.

He shifted so she could feel his erection. "I would like nothing more than to lock ourselves in my room for a day or two for starters, but I have somewhere to be." He pulled back. "Hey, why don't you come with me?"

Tilly straightened the collar of his shirt. "Where are you going?"

"There's a shelter downtown Knox mentioned might be a fit for a trial run of the charitable division."

She'd helped him brainstorm how to make his proposal impossible to refuse. In fact, he wanted to ask her to partner with him and work for Benedict Industries, but he was afraid she'd think he was moving too fast.

"Of course." She hopped out of his lap, and he resisted the urge to pull her back. "Let me go change."

They took his car, and Tilly recognized the location immediately. "I'm guessing it's not a coincidence this shelter is also near the port terminal Kipling was at and Mandy was found."

"Nope." Keaton parked the car and came around to her side to help her out. "I thought we could look around. I know the police already did their investigation, but you and I both know how I feel about the local police, aside from Alyssa."

"Are we snooping before or after we visit the shelter?"

"After, I think."

They were met inside the shelter by a frazzled looking man with unkept hair and disheveled clothing. He shook their hands and led them down dark hallways into an office cluttered with boxes. Only a few of the boxes were opened.

"What is all this?" Keaton asked as the man moved several boxes off a threadbare couch in the office.

The man scratched his head and shrugged. "Donations? I don't have time to look through it all."

The phone on the desk rang and he picked it up. "Hello?"

Keaton caught Tilly's gaze and lifted his eyebrows. *Can you believe this mess?*

"I'm so sorry," the man said, interrupting their silent conversation. "We've had issues today and I need to take care of a few things. I'll be right back"

Keaton assured him it was fine. After the guy left and closed the door, Tilly leaned toward Keaton.

"I can't believe it's only today they've had issues," she said. "I've never seen so much disorganization in one place."

"Agreed," he said, making notes on his phone. "They need someone with some top notch managerial skills to come in and take over."

Tilly stood. "I think I'll go see what they have as far as women and children's services. I believe I saw a reception area to the side when we first came in."

It was on his tongue to tell her to be careful, but he refrained. Besides, what trouble could she get into at a homeless shelter?

"You know this place was once a funeral home?"

Tilly turned at the question and found a teenager standing by a door marked 'Staff Only.' The girl was dressed all in black with black lipstick and black hair. But what struck Tilly the most were her empty looking eyes.

"Really?" Tilly glanced down the hall, the reception desk wasn't too far, but someone was being helped at the moment. "That's kinda creepy."

"There wasn't any equipment left here, but there's a room downstairs they used to do the embalming in. It has a particular smell, that room."

"Jade!" A sharp voice stopped the teen from saying anything further. A resident, if Tilly had to guess, but she didn't want to make assumptions. Although she doubted an employee would wear such a huge hat. Tilly couldn't even see her face.

"You're needed in the kitchen," the hat lady told the teen.

Jade huffed before turning and walking away without speaking.

The lady waited until the young woman was out of sight. "Sorry about that, teenagers, you know?"

"Yes, I most certainly do," Tilly said and waited for the woman to disclose the real reason she'd sent the teen away.

"I saw you come in with that man." She looked around and motioned for Tilly to follow her to a nearby room.

"Um." Tilly glanced over her shoulder to the office where Keaton waited. She didn't think the woman beckoning her into another room was dangerous, but the truth was, you never really knew. "I better stay here. I'd hate for him to finish his meeting and not know where I went."

The woman walked closer and out of instinct, Tilly looked down to make sure her hands were empty.

"Gracious," the woman said, holding her palms up. "Paranoid much?"

Tilly gave her a small smile and told her the truth. "I'm afraid so. It's been an interesting few weeks. I don't mean any offense."

"I understand. I have something I need to tell you, but can we step out of the line of sight for the front desk?"

"Back this way?" Tilly asked, heading back the way she came.

"Sure."

They walked down the hall until a storage cabinet blocked them from the sight of the front desk. It wasn't completely out of the way, but they were alone for the moment. Plus there were enough people nearby Tilly felt confident the woman wouldn't be able to try anything.

"What can I help you with?" Tilly asked.

"It's not what you can do for me. It's what I can do for you."

Tilly raised an eyebrow.

"That man you're with. He's one of those Benedict boys, isn't he?"

"Yes." Tilly couldn't think of a reason not to be truthful.

Their visit wasn't a secret and the Benedicts were known locally. Probably most of the shelter's residents knew who they were.

"I thought so. Handsome lot. All three of them."

Go on, Tilly wanted to say but didn't.

"Damn shame the way they're trying to pin that girl's murder on the oldest boy. Especially since he didn't do it." The woman spoke with a knowing grin, fully aware she now had Tilly's complete attention.

"Do you know something about what happened?" Tilly tried to remain calm but wasn't sure she carried it off.

"I know that girl was alive when Mr. Benedict left her. I was there. Or close enough anyway."

"And no one saw you?" Tilly asked.

"How often do you take note of the homeless?"

She had a point, but unfortunately, Tilly still didn't think it was enough to get the charges against Kipling dropped. "Why haven't you told the police?"

"Because bad things happen around here, if you know what I mean."

"No," Tilly said, losing patience. She wasn't sure which she wanted to do more, shake the woman or hug her. "What do you mean things happen?"

The woman looked as if she couldn't believe she'd been asked to explain. With a half roll of her eyes, she leaned close to Tilly, and whispered, "People disappear from here all the time, especially after talking to the police."

Tilly forced herself to stay calm. As much as she wanted to believe she had an eye witness, she was also aware that every word could be a fabrication.

"I tell you what," Tilly said by way of a compromise. "Why don't you write down everything you saw and did that night? Mr. Benedict and I will be back tomorrow, and you can give it to us then."

The woman bit her bottom lip. "No, I can't."

Her hesitation made it more likely the story was a fabrication, after all. "Why?"

"How much press coverage do you think there is when a homeless person is murdered?"

She looked pointedly at Tilly as if she was trying to get her to understand the hidden meaning in her words. Tilly remembered how careful she'd been about not being seen. "Are you saying you're afraid someone's going to come after you? We can keep you safe. We can involve the police..." Tilly stop talking at the woman's laughter.

She adjusted her a hat and glanced over her shoulder. "There's no press coverage for dead homeless people, and if you involve the police, that's what I'll be. Dead."

Tilly recognized a will of steel when she saw one. It was doubtful she'd learn more.

"One more question," Tilly said, deciding to try anyway. "What were you doing by the docks that night?"

The other woman moved as if to walk past her, but Tilly grabbed her arm. "Tell me, or I get Mr. Benedict and we have this conversation at the police station."

She bit her lip. "It was nothing, really. I saw the Benedict guy there with the blonde and I thought maybe I could sell some pictures. I mean, they ended up not doing anything, but she got on her knees and for a minute or two it looked like she was going to blow him or something"

"You have *pictures?*" Tilly asked in disbelief.

"Shhh." The woman looked around. "I have an old cellphone. I don't have service or anything, but the camera works and no one seems to notice or care."

"But you have pictures? Of that night?" Tilly bit her lip to keep herself calm. "I need that cell phone."

Tilly's mind spun, trying to think of how they could get the phone. Did they beg her? Go to the police? Heck, if it'd prove Kipling's innocence, she'd break into the shelter at night and steal the damn thing.

Tilly tugged her toward the office. "At least come with me to get Keaton and tell him—"

A loud piercing siren interrupted her.

"Fire!" someone yelled.

A fucking fire alarm? Wasn't that just great? People poured out into the hall. Tilly couldn't smell smoke, but that didn't necessarily mean there wasn't a fire.

Where was Keaton?

"Tilly!"

She looked behind her and saw Keaton jogging her way. "Come on, we need to go."

Someone bumped into her hard, but she ignored them, wanting to keep her eyes on Keaton. There were so many people, she didn't want to lose him. Finally, he made it to her.

She pulled him to the side, away from the press of the crowd. "Keaton, you have to meet someone." But when she turned, the woman she'd been talking to was gone.

Across the hall, watching her and not appearing to be in any hurry to make it outside, stood Jade, the teen with the empty eyes.

JADE

I learned early that my life would be easier if I followed a few simple rules.

-Don't interrupt King. Wait for him to acknowledge you before speaking.

-If you have to ask him for something don't do it when he's in a bad mood.

-Make sure it's a mountain you're willing to die on before telling him no.

I stood just inside the doorway of his office while he carried on a phone conversation. He knew I was there and that I'd wait to be acknowledged before speaking.

King ended his conversation and motioned me forward with a wave of his hand. I took a step farther inside and reached back to close the door behind me, but King held up his hand.

"Leave it open," he said.

I walked the few steps to stand in front of him. "I have an update for you."

His smile didn't reach his eyes, and the skin on the back of my neck prickled in warning.

"Wait a minute," he said. "Someone else will be joining us."

My mouth went dry and my head thumped with each beat of my heart. I had the strangest urge to run, but one look at King changed my mind. "Yes, sir," I managed to get out.

Seconds later, one of King's employees, Greg, walked in. For reasons I'd never been able to understand, most of King's men didn't like me, and Greg was no exception. Kevan was the only one who ever talked to me of his own free will.

"Sir," Greg said when he made it by my side.

King lifted a hand and his most experienced enforcer moved out from a dark corner. I was sure he had a name, but people who lived in the shadows didn't need one. All I knew was that the man was scary as fuck.

"It's a pity it's come to this," King said, but there was a joyful note in his voice that implied the opposite. "But only one of you can remain here."

Neither Greg nor I moved or spoke.

"Unfortunate, but necessary." King templed his fingers and looked over both of us before his gaze settled on Greg. "You start."

"Sir?" Greg asked and I risked a glance and saw his forehead dotted with sweat.

"Tell me again what you said this morning about the Benedict car and Jade," King said.

Fuck.

Greg swallowed and kept his focus on King. "After she trashed the apartment, she slashed the tires on Benedict's car."

"Is this true?"

I squared my shoulders at his question. "Yes, sir." Another rule I learned—don't ever lie. Had Kevan ratted on me? How did Greg know?

"Give me the knife you used." King held out his hand.

I carried three knives with me at all times. The one in question was my favorite, but I handed it to him.

"This isn't just any old, regular knife, is it?" King asked.

I couldn't tell if it was a rhetorical question or not. King knew the answer. "No, sir."

"In fact, it's so unique that someone with the knowledge of such things could see the difference between the cuts made with it compared to those made from a knife of lesser quality. Correct?"

"Yes, sir."

"When you slashed the tires," King continued. "You did more than disobey. You left behind evidence. Both of those are unacceptable."

I wouldn't be leaving King's office alive. I tried to accept my fate, but my brain rebelled. My throat closed, and I felt a sob of despair building in my chest.

Damnit. I wasn't going to cry. I wasn't.

King gave a low chuckle.

Fear.

He'd told me once he loved the smell of fear, that it made him happy and was his favorite scent. Seeing how much he seemed to be enjoying mine was the thing I needed to dry up any potential tears.

"Now, Jade," King said. "You said you had an update for me. Give it to me now."

Maybe my actions following that discovery would save me or at least buy some time. "Someone was on the docks taking pictures the night the dancer was killed. A homeless woman."

Greg gasped beside me. "No. That's not possible."

"You've already had your say," King said. "Continue, Jade."

"When I found out, I went to the shelter to see if I could find her." To the shelter's residents, I was Jade, a teen runaway who showed up every so often for a meal or a place to stay. "It wasn't hard. There was only one woman said to have a phone. No one else was ignorant enough to break that rule. I found her talking to Tilly Brock, who arrived with the younger Benedict, Keaton,

so I pulled the fire alarm. I didn't see her pass off the phone, but I can't find it, either."

King didn't praise me for my quick actions, nor did I expect him to do so. He simply nodded. "The woman claimed she never had a phone, but my men eventually persuaded her to tell the truth. As a reward, I graciously allowed her to pick her punishment. She chose to serve as entertainment to several of my clients instead of being alligator food."

I'd met King's clients before, and I'd witnessed enough of what they considered entertainment to know the better choice would have been to be fed to the alligators.

"Which means," King continued, "the gators are still hungry. Since I've decided to keep only one of you in my employment..." King looked over the two us standing before him. "Jade, you were sloppy, but I can appreciate the intent behind your actions. However, it better not happen again. Greg, you were not only sloppy, you let photographic evidence behind that will set me back for months."

I wasn't able to breath a sigh of relief because at that moment Greg began to sob and beg. I kept my gaze locked on a spot on the wall behind King while the enforcer restrained Greg and took him out of the room.

King didn't speak until everything was silent once more.

"My plans have changed," he said. "Tilly Brock is a problem, and your new assignment is to eliminate her."

CHAPTER 19

Keaton did the best he could to keep his eyes on the road as he and Tilly drove back to Benedict House. An act made difficult with the fantastical story Tilly shared about the homeless woman.

"We have to go back," Tilly said. "We have to get that cell phone."

Keaton tapped his fingers on the steering wheel, waiting for a stoplight to change. "I wonder if we should call the police and tell them. They could get a search warrant."

"I thought we both agreed we didn't trust anyone on the police department other than Officer Adams," Tilly argued. "And not only do we not know her name, she seemed really scared about going to the police. I'd hate if something happened to her because she talked to me"

As much as Keaton didn't want to, he agreed with her. "Okay, we'll go back tomorrow. Maybe that'll give the unnamed woman time to think, and she'll hand over the phone."

"I can't believe I didn't ask her name. She kept talking

about no one notices the homeless, and I didn't even get her damn name."

Keaton glanced out the side of his eyes to see a tear slip down Tilly's cheek. He put a hand on her knee. "Hey. You okay?"

Tilly nodded silently. "Yeah. I guess she affected me more than I thought. I can't imagine why she ran off the way she did."

"Maybe that Jade girl scared her." Keaton had caught a glimpse of the teen. He couldn't explain it, but she gave off a strange vibe that had nothing to do with the way she dressed and everything to do with the soulless look in her eyes.

"She seemed rather harmless."

Keaton kept his thoughts to himself.

They arrived at Benedict House not long after. He needed to type up his notes from the shelter meeting and work on the proposal for Kipling. Tilly said she needed to talk to Maggie.

"Meet you in the kitchen in an hour?" he asked as they walked inside. "I saw Maggie had picked up some ice cream. We should make banana splits."

It had been a favorite summertime treat to share when they were kids. He drank in the sight of her first smile since they'd left the shelter.

"Yes," she said. "Definitely."

Kipling was working in the downtown office for the day, so Keaton took over the home office. He'd just turned on his laptop when Tilly flew inside, her eyes wide with excitement and something clutched in her hand.

"She must have dropped it in my bag when she bumped into me," Tilly said.

"The phone?" He stood. "Really?" He didn't want to get his hopes up but felt them rise anyway.

His breath caught at the cell phone she lifted. It was an old model he knew wasn't made anymore and hadn't been for years.

"Yes." She nodded in excitement. "I can't believe it."

"Have you looked yet?"

"No," she said. "It's off, and I wanted to talk to you first."

He held out his hand. "Come here. Let's plug it into the laptop and see what we have."

She clutched the phone to her chest. "Be there. Be there. Be there."

He raised an eyebrow.

"It helps," she said. "Like hitting refresh repeatedly."

Her hands shook as she handed him the phone. He took hold of her. "You know no matter what's on this, that everything's going to be okay?"

"Yes." She sighed. "I just know he's innocent. There has to be a way to prove it."

He pulled her close and rested his chin on the top of her head. "We both know he didn't do it. Even if this doesn't hold what we hope it does, we have to believe the truth will come out some way."

"What if it doesn't?"

He dropped his voice. "I can't think that way. I have to believe our justice system works. In putting away the guilty *and* acquitting the innocent."

"I have zero faith in our justice system."

"Let's not wait any longer, then." He pulled away, and neither one of them talked while he moved the memory card from phone to laptop.

He scrolled through the files until he came to the pictures.

"Be there. Be there. Be there," Tilly started chanting again as he opened the file.

An image of Kipling walking alone away from the dock was the last picture taken.

"That fits with her story she only wanted pictures of Kipling having sex," Keaton said. "Too bad she didn't care about what Mandy was doing. If she had been, maybe we'd have a shot of the real killer."

He moved to the previous picture and there it was. Tilly squealed and starting jumping up and down.

"I knew it! I knew it! I knew it!" she sang.

Keaton couldn't help beaming at her excitement, even as he kept his eyes glued to the image of Kipling walking away from Mandy, on her knees in the background.

"They could say he came back and killed her." Keaton hated to bring it up, but he had to be realistic. "All this really proves is he was walking away at *that* point. There's nothing to prove he didn't turn around right after the last picture was taken and kill her then."

Tilly stopped jumping. "True, but it's *something* right?"

"Enough for a jury to find reasonable doubt, yes, I would think so. But enough to get charges dropped? Probably not."

"It's more than we had five minutes ago."

"Agreed. It's definitely worth giving to the cops and, who knows, maybe they'll have better luck with our mystery woman than you did."

While he'd been talking, Tilly had moved to stare at the computer screen. "Do we know how Mandy was killed?" she asked.

"No, they haven't released that."

"If it was a knife like the other two, we're in luck."

He spun around to look at the picture again. "What?"

Tilly increased the size of the photo, distorting it slightly. She punched a few keys and pulled up the original resolution and put the two images side by side.

"See this?" she asked, pointing to the shadowy image of a man walking toward Mandy, coming from the opposite side, and behind Kipling.

"Yeah."

"If you blow it up, there's something in his hand. It kind of looks like a knife."

Keaton looked at the photo and squinted his eyes. It might be a knife. Or did it only look like one because he wanted it so badly? "It might be a knife."

"Come on." Tilly punched him. "What else could it be?"

"I don't know. Let's call Officer Adams and give the photo to her."

"You're right. I know you are, but damn."

Keaton put an arm around her. "Don't be upset. I want us to be completely certain before we start celebrating."

"Call her."

Keaton took his phone out of his pocket and dialed the number on the card Kipling had out on his desk. "Officer Adams," he said when she answered. "This is Keaton Benedict. I have a question for you."

"What can I help you with Mr. Benedict?" she asked.

"Was Mandy killed with a knife?"

There was silence on the other end of the phone. He heard a door close in the background.

"Why do you ask?"

"Because if she was, I believe we just found a picture of our killer."

"I think you better explain yourself, Mr. Benedict."

CHAPTER 20

Two days after he called Alyssa, Keaton sat in the living room with Kipling and Tilly, waiting for the police and Derrick to arrive.

"Where's your partner?" Kipling asked once Alyssa had arrived and been shown in by Maggie. "Don't you need him to be good cop? Or are you just going to entertain us with your bad cop impression? I have to warn you, I like it very, very bad."

Alyssa sat down beside him. "Your pathetic attempts to disarm me by using sexual innuendos aren't working."

Instead of being deterred at the fact Alyssa called him out on his behavior, Kipling's face lit with delight. "You know, I did a little checking. I was wondering why your name sounded so familiar. It would seem I'm not the only one who likes it bad."

"I don't know what you're talking about."

But even Keaton saw her face was more guarded than it'd been seconds before. His guess was she knew exactly what Kipling was talking about and desperately wanted to change the subject.

Unfortunately, Kipling noticed the same thing. His older brother leaned back into his seat, the very picture of a man used to being in charge. "Tell me, Officer Adams. How is it possible for an officer of the law not to know, or at least suspect, that her lover is a murdering sex trafficker?"

The question was so preposterous Keaton waited for Alyssa to volley an insult back. Instead, she looked him straight in the eye and calmly said, "Love is blind, Mr. Benedict. Haven't you heard?"

"Perhaps. But I hadn't realized it was stupid as well."

Alyssa's lips tightened. "I don't see how my past relationship has anything to do with my current investigation."

"That's where you're wrong, Officer. It has everything to do with the current investigation. How do you expect me to believe you can tell which end's up when you didn't even know the man you were sleeping with had blood on his hands?"

Shocked at the turn the conversation had taken, Keaton tried to remember a news story even remotely related to what was being discussed. Damn. He had no idea. That's what he got for not ever watching the news.

The corner of Alyssa's mouth quirked up. "Did you realize who I was when you first saw me or did you have to Google me?"

There were relatively few people who gave to Kipling as good as they got. Keaton hadn't expected the police office to be one of them. His older brother obviously felt the same. He laughed and replied, "Touché, Officer Adams. Touché."

Alyssa, on the other hand, didn't look even mildly amused. "I know your type, Mr. Benedict. You think you're better than everyone else because you're wealthy. You think if something doesn't go your way, you can just buy your way out. Well, guess what? Newsflash. I'm not for sale."

"For the record, I'm not just wealthy. I'm insanely wealthy. And guess what? Newsflash. Everyone is for sale. Even you. All I have to do is find your price." His voice dropped a notch. "Would you like for me to try? Rumor has it I'm very thorough when it comes to something I want to buy."

Alyssa's cheeks flushed. She had to hate that. "I'm not interested, Mr. Benedict."

An uncomfortable silence followed. Derrick broke it by walking into the living room. "Sorry I'm late. What's going on?"

Alyssa snapped back to attention. "All charges against Kipling have been dropped. It's been verified the knife in the picture the unknown man is holding is the type that killed not only Mandy, but Mindy, and the bartender as well. It's not enough to convict the man in the picture, but it's enough to let Kipling go."

It was the news they expected, but they let up a cheer anyway. Keaton took Tilly's hand and mouthed, *You did it.*

She squeezed back. *We all did.*

Derrick looked pointedly at Alyssa. "You're relatively free with the information."

If he expected an apology, there wasn't one forthcoming. "I don't see eye to eye with the Charleston PD on a lot of things pertaining to this case," Alyssa said. "And it's my job to see justice done. Unfortunately, the two don't seem to line up all the time. They wanted me to hold off on dropping the charges a few more days, but I didn't see the point. He is innocent, after all."

"Told you I didn't do it." His older brother's smug side was back in full force. That he'd lost it at all meant he hadn't been as certain of the outcome as he'd acted.

"You were very lucky," Derrick said. "And don't you forget about it."

"I'm a Benedict. We don't believe in luck."

"Call it whatever you want then. Most of the time, proof of innocence doesn't just fall into your lap. Or in this case, into your purse," Alyssa finished with a nod toward Tilly.

Keaton knew Tilly enough to know something was still bothering her.

"What is it?" Keaton asked, dropping his voice.

"Have they been able to find the woman who took the pictures?" Tilly asked. "I can come by the shelter and help."

"I can go with you," Keaton said.

"You don't have to."

"I want to. They still haven't been to track down the person responsible for trashing your apartment and threatening you."

"I'm sure they have more important things to do," Tilly said. "Like figuring out who really killed the twins and Raven."

"I'm no investigator," Kipling said. "But I'm guessing it was the guy in the picture."

"You know what I meant," Tilly shot back.

"Doesn't matter," Kipling said. "It no longer involves the Benedicts or you, so we can step aside and let the Charleston PD do its job."

"Is this a family meeting I wasn't invited to?"

Their heads turned at the sound of Knox's voice. He stood in the hallway leading to the front door, and he looked mad as hell. Beyond that, there were dark bags under his eyes suggesting numerous sleepless nights.

"Knox," Kipling said. "Come sit down and join us."

"Nice to see you're back to treating everything like a joke now that you're no longer the prime suspect, asshole."

Knox stormed into the room and stopped directly in front of Kipling. "Are you forgetting that we still don't know who attacked Bea?"

Kipling stood so he was eye-to-eye with his brother. "I may be an asshole, but the one thing I take seriously is family, and the second some bastard left Bea to die on our property, she became my business. So don't talk to me about what I do and do not care about."

A new voice came from the hall.

"What the hell is going on in here?"

All eyes turned to the doorway where a pissed off Elise stood.

"Fuck," Knox said.

Keaton glared at her. "Elise, this doesn't concern you. Leave."

Elise pointed to Tilly. "She gets to stay."

"Now," Keaton said in a low and cold voice.

Elise shot Tilly a death glare, then turned and left the room. Kipling took a deep breath. "Keaton, that girl has become a problem. Deal with her tonight or I will."

Keaton had actually planned to talk to Elise tonight. He'd known the conversation was going to really upset her, but now...hell, had no idea what she'd do. "I'll talk with her."

"Sounds like you're in for an interesting conversation tonight," Tilly whispered.

"We knew it was coming."

Seemingly satisfied, Kipling shifted his attention to the plain clothes officer in his living room. "Officer Adams, I know it's hard for you to stay away from me, but I doubt you want to listen to our family drama. I can walk you out if you're not ready to say goodbye to me just yet."

"I actually do have more information for you," Alyssa

said. "We have a name of the mysterious picture-taking woman. Her name is Evelyn Dubious. She's twenty-nine and has lived at the shelter for about two months. Other residents describe her as quiet, helpful, and usually keeps to herself. I know you only had the one conversation with her, Ms. Brock, but does this sound like the woman you talked with?"

"Sure," Tilly said. "But the same could be said about a lot of people. Why don't I meet you at the station or the shelter so I can see her?"

Keaton didn't miss Alyssa's wince, and he moved his hand to Tilly's knee. He had the feeling she would need his support following whatever Alyssa said next.

"Unfortunately, Ms. Dubious hasn't been seen following the false fire alarm."

A faint shudder shook Tilly, but she didn't say anything immediately. When she did speak, she didn't sound surprised. "I think she knew the fire alarm was fake. She'd insinuated she'd be in trouble if she told me too much."

"We've confirmed the alarm pulled was the one closest to where you were standing."

"In that case, you may want to talk to a teenager named Jade. She was hanging around watching us," Tilly said. "I mean, I don't want to go around making accusations, but she seemed a bit...*off* to me."

"You're not the first person to mention her, and we'd like to talk to her as well. Interestingly enough, she hasn't been seen since the false alarm either."

Keaton shifted in his seat. "How long had Jade been at the shelter?"

"She comes and goes," Alyssa said. "No one I spoke to knows much about her. They said she doesn't talk a lot about herself."

There had to be somewhere else they could look. Keaton was grateful they had the camera, but surely there was more.

"Security cameras," Keaton said as the idea popped into his head. "They're all up and down the docks. What are the odds they might have captured the killer?"

"Fairly good, actually," Alyssa said. "In fact, there's one positioned to record the exact spot Mandy was standing. Unfortunately, they were all shot out days before her death."

"Someone's good," Kipling said. "And knows what they're doing. You better hope you're half as good."

"Trust me, Mr. Benedict, I'm very good at what I do. Very, very good." Said by any other woman, it would have come across as a come on but not when spoken by her.

"That remains to be seen," Kipling added, appearing not at all ready for their verbal foreplay to come to an end. "But I have to say one thing."

Alyssa had shifted and leaned forward. Probably unknowingly.

Kipling smiled. "As much as the thought of you holding a gun turns me on, remind me never to get on your bad side."

"Too late." She stood. "You reside there permanently."

"Do you have any further questions for any of my clients?" Derrick asked.

"No, I was getting ready to leave."

Derrick struggled to his feet, using his arms to help lift his weight from the chair. "I'll walk out with you."

Keaton wondered if he had really intended to leave then or if he adjusted his plan once Alyssa announced she was leaving. They didn't appear to be talking as they left, but

Kipling had a better view of the front door from where he sat.

Too bad all he was doing was staring at Alyssa's ass.

CHAPTER 21

Tilly's hand drifted across Keaton's thigh, and he sucked in a breath. They had planned to review details Knox had pulled about missing residents of the homeless shelter to see if there were any similarities among them. Though now that Keaton thought about it, going over the lists on his bed probably wasn't the best way to be productive.

"Do you want to hand me that paper to your right?" he asked Tilly.

Her hand moved farther up his thigh, and she shifted so their lips were inches apart. "Not particularly."

"Mmm." He placed the paper he'd been reading aside and kissed her. "Who came up with the idea to look over all this in bed?" he asked against her lips.

"You." She pushed on his chest until he was on his back and she leaned over him. "I thought it was an incredibly brilliant idea."

It turned him on so much when she took charge. "You did?"

"Oh, yes." Her hands made quick work of his pants.

"I'm afraid I'm going to need more evidence of my brilliance," he teased.

She sat up, moved the papers, and with her eyes on his, striped her shirt off. She wasn't wearing a bra and didn't say anything, but rather, lifted an eyebrow.

"Damn, I'm a genius."

"I am, too," she said with a wickedly sexy smile. "Want to know why?"

"Tell me."

"I'm not wearing underwear either. Want to see?"

God, he loved it when she was playful. When she teased him the way she was doing now. "I want to see so badly."

He'd thought she'd drag it out and make him wait. Or at least make him beg. But to his relief, she must have wanted him as much as he wanted her. And like him, she didn't seem to want to practice delayed gratification.

"Watch," she said as if it were possible for him to do otherwise.

She was so beautiful, he could only nod and when she lifted herself to her knees to shimmy down her shorts; it took all he had not to help. But even more than he wanted her naked, he wanted to watch her. She took his breath away.

There were no more clothes between them. When she lowered herself on him with her gaze firmly on his, and as she began to slowly ride him, he kept his hands on her hips and let her lead them both to pleasure.

Only when her climax hit did she close her eyes and throw back her head. Her release triggered his, and he didn't hold back, but let it wash over him. For those few precious moments, there was nothing in their world except the two of them.

As their breathing returned to normal, she rested with

her head on his chest. "Are you really going to talk to Elise tonight?"

"Yes," he said. "I've put it off as long as I can."

"Will you do it here or go out somewhere?"

"I'm not going out in public with her and risk a big scene."

Tilly pushed up on her elbow. "Should I stay in the house or would it be best for me to leave?"

"I don't want you to leave. I'd like for you to stay here. Preferably with a weapon nearby, but you should probably forget the weapon because Derrick would probably have a heart attack."

She ran her hand down his chest and grinned at his sucked in breath. "Maybe we'll both be surprised at how well she takes it."

They caught each other's eyes and smiled at the same time. "Nah."

Keaton's smile faltered. "I can't decide if I'm making the best choice for the family, or if I'm being selfish." He leaned in for a kiss, only to be interrupted by a knock on the door.

"Keaton," Kipling said. "This was not what I had in mind when I said to take care of the situation."

Keaton groaned. "I'm coming."

"There's a joke in there somewhere, but I'm not touching it," Kipling said.

"He didn't just go there, did he?" Tilly asked.

"Hey, Tilly," Kipling said through the door.

She blushed, and it was beautiful. "Hey, Kip."

"I'm walking away now," Kipling said. "I have to stop by the office. Apparently, a pipe burst, and there's water all over the floor."

"Trade ya," Keaton said.

"Not going to happen. Get your ass out of bed."

Keaton rolled out of bed after giving Tilly one last kiss. She flopped back and pulled the sheet up to her chin.

"I'm going to stay right here and keep your spot warm," she said.

Keaton pulled on the pair of jeans he'd thrown on the floor and buttoned up the shirt Tilly removed hours before. He wasn't sure if Elise was still in the house. If so, she knew exactly what he'd been doing since Alyssa and Derrick left.

Probably wasn't the best idea, telling her to go to hell after leaving Tilly's embrace. On the other hand, it could be seen as the ultimate "fuck you."' Either way you looked at it, though, one thing was almost certain. It wasn't going to be pretty.

He stepped into his bathroom and made himself as presentable as possible. He had to do this. To even think about giving into Elise's demands meant a lifetime of bowing to her wishes. He would never allow her to have that kind of power over him. He'd rather die than spend the rest of his life being her beck-and-call boy.

The door to the bathroom was open, and through it, he saw Tilly. She'd grabbed a novel she'd left on his nightstand and was reading. Naked. He watched mesmerized as she lifted a hand to her head to push a lock of hair behind her ear. His eyes followed her finger as it dropped to the book to turn the page. He'd kissed that finger no more than an hour ago and yet, he still wanted more. He would always need more when it came to Tilly.

She was the main reason he was going to tell Elise where she could stuff it. He knew in his heart saying yes to Elise was the same as saying no to Tilly. It meant giving up Tilly, and he never planned to give her up again.

Suddenly, he didn't want to see Elise without Tilly knowing exactly how he felt. He needed her to understand she owned his heart. Was it too soon for him to tell her he loved her?

Maybe.

Was there a possibility she wouldn't say it back?

Of course.

Did he care?

Not one bit.

She sat up and reached for him as he walked into the room. Going into her arms was as easy as breathing, and once there, he was home.

He took her hands tightly in his. "I love you, Tilly Brock."

A few tears ran down her cheeks, and he put his arms around her, crushing her to him. "Don't cry, baby. Please."

She sniffed. "They're happy tears. Because I love you, too."

He felt as if his heart would bust right out of his chest. She loved him.

She. Loved. Him.

He damn near floated out of the room.

ELISE HAD SHUT herself in her room, but he was ready to get this over with and knocked on the door.

"Who is it?" Elise asked from within.

He rolled his eyes. "It's me." Seriously, who else would it be?

"Come in."

He cracked the door open. She'd lit candles. He pushed the door open a bit more. Elise stood off to the side of the bed, wearing a skimpy, silky robe.

Jesus. She had been expecting him.

But there was more than lust staring back at him with her eyes. Anger simmered not too far below the surface.

She put her hands on her hips. "You have some nerve coming here after leaving that slut in your bed. You should have showered first. You smell like her."

Rage surged through him. "If you were a man, I'd have knocked your teeth down your throat for talking about Tilly like that." He took a deep breath to calm down. The best thing he could do was to get away from her as quickly as possible. "I've made a decision."

A look of victory crossed her face, but only temporarily. Her eyes narrowed as she guessed exactly what he'd decided. "Go on."

"I'm not going to marry you," he said as calmly as possible. "And I don't care what evidence you fling around or who you attempt to set up with what."

Whatever she was expecting, that wasn't it. "You're going to regret that decision."

"I really don't think so."

"You will. I'll see to it."

"Knox and Kipling don't even know we had a younger sister. How do you think you'll get a murder charge to stick?"

"You'd be wise not to underestimate me."

He had a sinking feeling she was right, but even more so, he knew he couldn't live with the alternative. Just looking at her made him sick to his stomach. Is that what she really wanted in a life partner?

"Elise," he said, thinking it might help to reason with her. "You're a beautiful, successful woman. You could have your choice of men. You don't need me."

"You don't get it, do you?"

"Apparently not. Why don't you explain it to me."

"You're a Benedict, I'm a Germain. Our families are powerhouses separate, but together we could rule the world."

"Yeah, see," he said, "I have no need for that much power. "

"Of course, you don't. You've never been aware of your full potential. That's what makes Kipling so mad. You have everything you need, and you simply don't care."

How fucking dare she? "Don't bring Kip into this. I know for a fact he'd never want me to marry without love."

She laughed as if he'd just told the funniest joke she'd ever heard. "Love? Honestly, Keaton, you sound like a teenage girl. Your concept of marriage is so misguided. Marriage is about alliances, power, and bloodlines."

"You would set aside love and marry for power?" He knew not all marriages were rooted in love, but after feeling what he did for Tilly, he couldn't imagine settling for anyone other than his soulmate.

"I'm fond of you, but I don't believe in love." Anger flashed in her eyes again. "Don't take that to mean you can keep fucking Tilly once our engagement is announced. That shit stops now, understand?"

"Understand what? I just told you I wasn't marrying you."

"Because your thinking is all messed up. You're convinced in happily ever afters and rainbows and unicorns. Why do you think the divorce rate is so high? I'll tell you. Because everyone's bought into this 'love conquers all' bullshit. If people were more logical, everyone would be happier."

"I think that has to be one of the saddest things I've ever heard." He didn't want to think about how he might have actually agreed with her before Tilly came back into his life. But now that she had, he knew better. He knew love was real and, more importantly, he knew he didn't want to live without it. "And if you truly believe those words, you have to be the saddest person on the planet."

"I think you have love and sex confused. I may not love you, but I think we'll have a lot of fun in the bedroom." She slipped her robe down one shoulder. "Come here and let me show you how good it could be."

Before he knew what she was doing, the robe fell from the other shoulder onto the floor. In less time then it took him to blink, Elise stood naked before him.

He refused to look anywhere other than her eyes. "Put your clothes back on."

"Grow up. This isn't about anything other than biology. I spread my legs, and you use your dick to make us both happy."

But it was so much more. Biology was cold and clinical, and if that's what Elise thought sex was, he felt sorry for her. However, he wasn't going to be the one to show her the difference.

"God, you are such a child," she finally said at his refusal to look below her neck. She bent and put on her robe. When she finally looked at him he was surprised to discover she no longer looked angry; she looked resolved and, frankly, her resolve worried him more.

She methodically went to each candle and blew it out, turning on a lamp as she passed. When she spoke, there was no emotion in her voice. "I'd hoped you'd see things my way after I explained everything to you. I see now that I misjudged you. You're actually far weaker than I imagined. My offer still remains, though, if you decide you'd like to change your mind. If not, you can't say you weren't warned." She shooed him away like a fly. "Go on. Get out of my room."

"Elise."

"I mean it. Now.

He had the strange feeling that he shouldn't turn his back to her. But after what he'd just told her, he couldn't very well stay in her room. He turned and walked out of the room, telling himself he'd done what needed to be done.

It didn't make him feel any better.

He made it to his room and found Tilly still reading in bed. She looked at him with a million questions in her eyes, but he found he couldn't answer them at the moment. He held out his hand. "Come walk with me? I have to get out of this house."

Relief flooded him as she simply nodded and took his hand.

JADE

I sank back deeper into the shadows when Keaton and Tilly stepped outside into the lush garden surrounding the massive house. They spent a few minutes talking, their conversation so intense they were oblivious. Now would be the perfect time to make my move.

I had one job. Kill Tilly.

I couldn't do it.

Still coming to terms with that fact, I could do nothing but watch when the couple started kissing, and shortly thereafter, made their way back inside. I was one breath away from leaving my hiding spot when a nearby movement made me freeze.

A woman cursed and appeared from the shadows to my right. Someone else had been watching the couple. Even in the darkness, I saw the anger on the stranger's face and felt the heat of her hatred.

King would not like it if he learned of my inability to detect someone beside me, and he could never find out. After what happened to Greg, it was clear King now thought of me as expendable. Interestingly enough, it didn't bother me the way it should.

Instead, I felt free for the first time in my life.

CHAPTER 22

The next Saturday morning, Tilly went with Keaton to the downtown offices of Benedict Industries. Much to Kipling's delight, Keaton had picked out an office space. He'd asked her to help him decorate, and though she knew nothing about interior design, she'd jumped at the chance to help.

"I thought you didn't have any experience decorating," Keaton said in a half-teasing, half-serious voice after she'd shot down his third choice of paint color.

"I don't," she replied, ensuring her tone matched his. "As it turns out, I'm just really, really opinionated."

"And bossy," he said, this time smiling. "Can't forget bossy."

"I thought you agreed with me that the second color you liked looked like dried snot?"

"Of course I did." He was walking toward her slowly with a predatory grin. "How could I ever see it as anything else after you so eloquently described it?"

"And this last one reminds me of vomit." She pointed to

the brownish-orange color she hoped he'd been joking about liking.

"Does everything come back to a body fluid for you?" He'd reached her now, and grabbed her from behind, kissing the back of her neck.

"No," she said, reaching for the perfect yellow color swatch. "I call this one 'happy'. It makes me smile when I look at it."

"Hmm. It is a pretty color, but I wonder if it'd be better suited for that office." He pointed to an empty office adjoining his.

"Your admin's office?"

"No, I'm not going to have an admin."

"Oh?"she asked with mischief in her eyes. She knew he was up to something, but obviously had no idea what

"I've been thinking." He turned her to face him and ran his hands up and down her arms while he spoke. "You don't have to give me an answer today. And I don't want you to feel any obligation or pressure to say yes." He took a deep breath. "I'd like for you to come work with me."

"What?"

"I think you'd be the perfect partner for me and the charity division of Benedict Industries. I know you've been thinking about going back to school, but you can do both. At least say you'll think about it." He dropped his head to whisper, "And if you say yes, I have the most perfect paint color in mind for your office."

Her most recent plan was to schedule and take as many classes as possible, either online or somewhere local, to complete her degree as soon as possible. But she couldn't deny the appeal of Keaton's offer. She'd be able to help so many people as an employee of Benedict Industries. That was what she wanted to do, help people. She could still finish her degree, it'd just take a little longer.

"There have to be a lot of people more qualified than I am."

"I don't know their heart. I know yours, and you'd be prefect." He kissed her forehead. "Don't feel like you have to give me an answer today. Take your time and think about it." He pulled back. "Would you like to see your office?"

"Trying to sway me?"

"Whatever it takes." The predatory grin was back, and he reached out to take her hand. "I think you'll like it."

They had almost made to the empty office when her phone buzzed with an incoming text.

"Ignore it," Keaton whispered.

"I can't," she said, reaching into her pocket for her phone. "What if it's someone important?"

"I'm not important?"

"You are, but...oh my god." She checked the number to make sure she read it right. She held the phone up. "It's Bea."

What does she say?"

She read the text. "She needs to talk and wants to know if I'll meet her at Benedict House."

Keaton frowned. "I talked to Knox last night and he still hadn't heard from her. She's not returning any of his calls or messages. Do you think this is a positive sign?"

"I don't know. I really don't know her all that well. Maybe she found some information about the key."

"It's possible."

"Want to come with me?"

"No." He shook his head. "You take the car, and when you finish, come back and we'll go to lunch."

A minute later, he kissed her goodbye and helped her into the car. "Text me if you can to let me know how it's going."

AN HOUR LATER, Keaton couldn't get Tilly to reply to his texts. It shouldn't bother him. Hopefully, it meant her talk with Bea was going well. Maybe he'd turn around in ten minutes and see them walking into the office.

But when the front office door opened, it was only Knox. Keaton lifted a hand in greeting and looked at the clock. Maybe the talk wasn't going well, and she didn't want to tell him. That made sense, actually.

He walked into the office he'd claimed for her. It would look terrific painted her happy color. He shuffled through a few paint swatches trying to pick a color that complemented it, but put them back down, deciding it'd probably be better to wait until she got back. That way she couldn't tease him about how everything he picked out looked like a body fluid.

The phone in Knox's office rang, and his brother's voice floated down the short hallway as he answered. Keaton would wait and tell him about offering Tilly a job when he got off the phone.

Restless, he walked to the front door and looked out the windows. No Tilly. Nothing. He typed out another text.

Call me.

He deleted it before sending. He didn't want her to think he was controlling or trying to dictate her every move. He typed out another text.

Getting worried. LMK you're okay.

There. That was better.

Except she didn't call. He had to do something or else he'd start pulling his hair out. He went down the hall to Knox's office. His brother was still on the phone, but he lifted his hand and mouthed, *Give me one minute.*

Keaton couldn't wait a minute. He shook his head. *Off. Now.* He mouthed back.

Knox recoiled slightly, but ended his call. "What's wrong?" he asked. "And where's Tilly? I thought she was going to be with you today."

"That's what I wanted to talk to you about. Can you give me Bea's phone number?"

Knox's jaw tightened, then relaxed. Keaton let out a deep breath. That went better than he'd thought it would. But Knox's reply brought him to his knees.

"I can, but it won't do any good. Her phone was stolen the day she was attacked. Her brother told me. Talking to him is the way I can get information about her."

For a long moment, Keaton couldn't move, couldn't talk. He kept seeing himself kissing her goodbye and her excitement as she drove off. Would that be the last time he kissed her? He refused to let himself think that.

"Keaton?"

He realized Knox had gotten out of his chair and was standing in front of him only when he shook him slightly.

"You're scaring me, man," Knox said. "What's wrong?"

"Tilly got a text from Bea asking her to meet her at the house." Keaton was going to be sick. She'd been gone for an hour, and he'd done nothing. Nothing. He snatched Knox's keys from the top of his desk. "Come with me. She's been gone for an hour and has my car. I'm driving yours."

"I'll call the police on the way. We don't know who's meeting her there."

She'd been gone for an hour and hadn't returned any text or call. Whoever she was meeting, it was probably too late. He shook himself. No, he wouldn't allow himself to think that. He had to believe she was okay, because nothing made sense without her.

CHAPTER 23

Tilly stepped out of the car at Benedict House and noticed it was the only one in the driveway. Before Tilly had left, she'd sent a text to Bea asking where to meet but never received a response. Surely, Bea hadn't left. Tilly sent another, letting Bea know she'd arrived and asking if she was inside or outside in one of the gardens.

Minutes later, she still hadn't received a response. She sighed, deciding to look around. There was no one on the front porch, so she walked around to the side of the house. There were several nooks and crannies where a couple could sit and talk, but they were all empty. The bulk of the gardens were located in the backyard. She looked around quickly, but found no trace of Bea.

It made more sense for her to wait inside, anyway. Tilly let herself in and dropped her purse in the foyer. She peeked into the living room. Empty.

She frowned. "Bea?" Nothing. Maybe she hadn't arrived yet, but it seemed strange Bea would want to meet somewhere she wasn't.

Bea definitely wasn't in the house. Tilly sighed. She

would have stayed with Keaton longer if she'd known she'd have to wait. She reached for her phone to text and ask Bea what time she expected to be at the house, but her pockets were empty. Of course they were. She'd shoved her phone in her purse before leaving them both in the foyer.

She went into the hallway to get her purse but detoured to the kitchen to see if Maggie had seen or heard from Bea. Usually, she could hear Maggie doing something. The Benedict housekeeper loved to sing even though she couldn't stay on key to save her life. Today the kitchen was strangely quiet.

Thinking about Maggie brought a smile to Tilly's face. The older woman reminded her so much of her mother. She was grateful for their newly rekindled friendship.

"Hey, Maggie." Tilly stepped in to the kitchen.

And screamed.

Maggie was on the floor of the kitchen, clutching her belly, a pool of blood slowly spreading under her. At the sound of Tilly screaming, Maggie's eyes open in fear. Tilly dropped to her knees at her side.

"Hold on. I'm going to call for help." Tilly glanced around the kitchen, but there was no landline in the spacious room. "My phone's in the foyer. I'll just be a second."

"Run." It sounded as if Maggie used every ounce of strength she possessed to force out the word.

A shiver of fear ran down her spine at the realization whoever shot Maggie could still be in the house. Damn it. Why had she left her phone in foyer?

"Run," Maggie repeated. Her eyelids fluttered closed.

"Maggie?" Tilly shook her shoulder just a little, but the older woman's eyes remained closed. She felt for a pulse, breathing out a sigh of relief at the faint beat under her finger. "Hang in there. I'll be right back."

"I wouldn't count on it," said a cold and familiar voice from behind her.

She turned slowly and came face-to-face with a 9mm, held by a grinning Elise.

TILLY SLOWLY STOOD, her hands raised to show they were empty. "You shot Maggie?"

"Totally unplanned, but yes."

"Why?"

"Because she found the suicide letter I typed for you." Elise plucked a folded piece of paper from her pants pocket and cleared her throat. "Keaton, I'm sorry. I don't know what to say other than that. I didn't want it to come to this, but my choices caught up with me, and I'm afraid there's no other way for this to end. Before I go, I have to clear my soul. I'm the one who killed the twins and the bartender. They deserved it, and I won't apologize for it."

Elise paused. Perhaps waiting for Tilly to compliment her on her flawless prose. It wasn't happening. Tilly tightened her lips.

Elise glared at her while continuing to read. "My one regret is leaving you behind, but I am comforted knowing I never deserved you in the first place. I hope you find happiness."

"He'll never believe I wrote that." Tilly couldn't believe she was even capable of speech. Was she really standing in the Benedict's kitchen being read a suicide note someone had written for her, all the while, one of the sweetest women she ever met bleed out on the floor *and* her childhood best friend was holding a gun to her head?

Where was everyone? Lately, there were always a ton of people around the house, why was it so quiet today?

Her brain hadn't yet come to terms with the reality of the situation, she supposed. Once it did, she'd probably completely freak out. If she was still alive.

"He'll have no other choice but to believe it," Elise was saying. "I need you to sign the note."

"Hell, no. If it didn't matter, you'd go ahead and shoot me." Tilly had no idea why she was talking to Elise, but she must be doing something right; after all, she hadn't been shot yet. *Keep her talking.* How long would Keaton wait before he got worried? If she didn't text the way he asked, would he know something was up?

"How did you get Bea's phone?" Tilly asked.

She didn't think Elise would answer, but she seemed quite proud of herself when she answered, "It fell out of her pocket when Keaton carried her from the foyer to the living room. I intended to give it back, but it was never brought up. I finally decided to keep it, thinking it might come in handy one day. I was right."

Tilly studied the woman before her, trying to see if any part of the girl she knew from childhood was hidden somewhere. When had she lost her humanity and who or what had taken it from her?

Elise motioned with the gun. "Go over to the table. This is taking too long. Someone's going to show up soon."

Tilly had never wanted Elise to be more right. *Please let someone be on their way.*

She needed to keep Elise talking. Compromise. Tilly stepped toward the table to buy time.

"Why?" Tilly asked as she slowly made her way across the kitchen. "Do you want Keaton so bad you feel you have to do this?"

"Keaton would be mine no matter what. Killing you is just the cherry on top." Elise flashed her pageant perfect smile. "He'll think you offed yourself, and I'll be there to put the pieces back together. He'll be so thankful, he'll propose."

There was no convincing her otherwise. Her twisted mind had somehow warped her brain into believing her lie.

"As to why him," Elise continued. "Money. I need it. Lots of it."

"But you're wealthy."

"No," Elise nearly shouted, showing anger for the first time since she'd lifted the gun to Tilly. "My family is wealthy. Namely, my father. But the bastard has cut me off. Said I needed to grow up and take some responsibility. Apparently, he wasn't impressed with the hacking I did to get into the university's system to change a few grades. He said I needed to explore my true potential. I'm not sure this is what he means, but it's what I'm doing. Getting you out of the way, so I can marry Keaton and have all this."

The puzzle pieces slowly started to fall into place. "Were you the one who trashed my apartment? And slashed Keaton's tires?" Tilly had to keep her talking. She glanced at the clock; she'd left Keaton about an hour ago. Surely, he was on his way. He had to know by now something was off.

Elise looked confused for the first time. "No."

They'd both made it to the table, and Tilly couldn't shake the feeling her time was up. Worse, there didn't seem to be anyone on the way to save her. If she was going to make it out of the kitchen alive, she was going to have to save herself.

Elise shoved the pen at her. "Sign it. Now."

What did she do? If she signed, would Elise shoot her

the second she finished? If she stalled, would Elise shoot her anyway?

Tilly's gaze drifted back to Maggie. If she focused enough, she thought she could make out the slow rise and fall of her chest. In a split second, she'd made her mind up.

"Call an ambulance for Maggie," Tilly said. "I'll sign anything you want, but don't let her die."

"I can't do that."

"Why?"

"She saw me. She can't live. In fact." Elise turned and pointed the gun at Maggie.

Tilly only had seconds to make a move. She took a step toward Elise when the world exploded around her.

JADE

My phone buzzed with a text. Damn it, what was it now?
But irritation turned to dread as I read.

He wants you in his office in five minutes.

There was no question who had summoned me, only why.
I stepped into the hallway and nearly tripped over someone.
"Watch where you're going, asshole."

"Jade," Kevan said. "Thank goodness I found you."

Surprised by the relief in his voice, I turned back to him.
"Why?"

Looking at him, I recalled how the first time I'd met him, I
didn't think he fit in with the rest of us. It was his eyes. They
weren't dead and empty. However, at the moment, they were
filled with fear.

"He's planing something," he spoke in a worried whispered.
"I don't know what, but it's bad and concerns you."

I couldn't move.

"You have to go." He glanced around the hallway. "Now.
Quickly. While he still thinks you're coming to him."

Through the years, I'd dreamed about running. Of getting away from King. Now it looked like today was the day. I hurried back into my room, making a list in my head of what I had and what I could easily fit in a backpack. I wouldn't be able to take everything I wanted, but that was okay, the important thing was to get away.

I took a deep breath even as excitement threatened to consume me. Clothes, I needed clothes, but not too many. Maybe three outfits? I shoved them in a backpack along with underwear.

I looked over my weapons, knowing I had to be careful with my selection. The guns weren't registered in my name. While that might be a good thing since they couldn't be traced to me, it was too cumbersome to travel with a gun these days. Knives, however... I was better with a knife anyway. I picked my four favorites, strapped one at my waist, shoved one into my boot, and packed the remaining two.

I took a careful step out into hallway. Kevan stood just outside my door. When he saw me, he shoved a bag in my hands. "Just some protein bars, apples, a couple bottles of water, and a few things you might find useful."

"Thanks." My cheeks heated. I couldn't remember the last time someone did something nice for me.

"Just be careful, Kaja." He held his hand out. "And give me your phone. There's a tracker in it."

Of course, there was. I dropped it into this outstretched hand, gave him a nod, and all but ran to the nearest door. For what felt like the first time, I stepped into the light.

I felt lighter with every step I took away from the dark house that had been both shelter and jail for as long as I could remember. It wouldn't last, eyes would be everywhere once he realized I had left for good. I should move far, far away.

A bus passed, filled with tourists. That was it, a bus. Cheap, yet effective. But I had one last thing to do before leaving the city for good. I had to warn the Benedicts.

It wasn't until I was almost at their house that I realized Kevan had called me by my real name.

CHAPTER 24

Keaton drove as fast as he could without being so reckless as to attract attention. Knox sat in the passenger seat, his hand anchored on the dash. He wouldn't say anything, perhaps being the only person who understood exactly how Keaton felt.

Inwardly, Keaton cursed himself. How could he not know Bea's phone had been lifted? How could he have let Tilly go so easily after what had happened to her apartment and the girls at the club? Damn it, if he wasn't the biggest idiot who'd ever walked the planet, he didn't know who was.

"Stop it," Knox said.

"What?"

"Beating yourself up over this." Knox moved his hand off the dash and settled back into the seat. "No matter what you think, this wasn't your fault."

Keaton scowled. "It is my fault, though. I just let her go off like it was nothing. I didn't even think."

"First of all, I know Tilly, and if you had told her she

couldn't go, she'd have told you to go to hell and went anyway."

Keaton couldn't help the chuckle. "Yeah, you're probably right."

"I know I am." Growing serious, Knox asked, "Who do you think it is?"

"I keep asking myself that question and, honestly, I don't know." But in his gut, he had a sinking suspicion he knew exactly who it was. Her voice taunted him over and over. *Don't say you weren't warned.*

He'd always thought she meant to harm him, not Tilly.

"You're doing it again," Knox said.

Keaton didn't see any reason to deny it, and they drove the rest of the way to the house in silence.

They pulled up to house. Everything was eerily quiet as they got out of the car. Typically, it would be quiet with all of them at work. But today, even the air seemed still. Waiting.

"Did you call the police?" Keaton asked.

"Yes. I don't know why they aren't here yet."

He and Knox decided to walk around the house and look inside windows to get a handle on the situation. Neither one of them wanted to say it, but there was a possibility Tilly wasn't at the house anymore. They split up. Keaton took the path winding through the garden, jogging. He planned to enter through a back window and hopefully have the element of surprise.

He turned a corner and froze.

"Who the hell are you?" He all but spit at the young woman standing in the very spot he was headed for. "What have you done to her? Where is she?"

But as he drew closer, he realized he knew her. The

young girl from the shelter. Except she was dressed in jeans today. "You," he said. "What are you doing here?"

He had to hand it to her. She didn't cower away from him. Instead, she seemed almost miffed he was there at all.

"Shhh." She pointed at the window. "Your girl is holding her own fairly well, but that crazy ass blonde will probably shoot her if they hear us."

Tilly?

He motioned to the girl, and she stepped out of the way, allowing him to peek into the kitchen. His relief at seeing Tilly alive lasted only a second because standing across the room holding a gun, was Elise. He lifted his hand to knock on the glass, but the stranger grabbed his wrist.

"Are you an idiot?" she whispered angrily. "Or do you want her dead?"

"It's Elise," he said, wondering why he was arguing with the teen. "She probably doesn't even know how to use a gun." He had to tell himself that or else he'd be ripping the window apart with his bare hands.

"Tell that to the lady on the floor."

He looked to where she pointed and choked back a sob at seeing Maggie's bloody body on the floor. His eyes flew back to Tilly. "We have to get her out of there."

The girl looked uncertain for the first time. "You just can't go charging in there. That blonde has all the power right now. You need a plan."

He ran his hand through his hair. He didn't have time for a plan. Elise had already shot Maggie. He'd never forgive himself if anything happened to Tilly.

"The plan is I get inside the house and get Elise's attention away from Tilly."

"How are you going to get inside?"

He'd had enough. "The back door. And I still don't know

who you are, but if you're still here when I get back, I'm having you arrested for trespassing."

"Listen to me. You can't go through a door, that's what she's expecting."

"You have any better ideas?"

"Yes, the secret passage that runs from the garden to the butler's panty."

He glanced through the window. Elise was still talking. He had to get in there. "Look, girl. I get that you're trying to be helpful, but I grew up in this house with two older brothers. Trust me. If there was a secret passage, I'd know about it."

She didn't say anything but simply grabbed his wrist again and pulled him away from the window and toward the back edge of the garden. She was surprisingly strong for someone of her size.

"What are you....I have get to Tilly...Damn it."

She stopped in front of an ivy-covered arbor and wiped her forehead. "Move it."

He wasn't sure why he obeyed, probably to prove her wrong, but he reached out and moved the arbor. His jaw dropped at the wooden door now freely exposed to the garden. "Holy shit."

She didn't look smug, she just nodded. "Leads straight to the butler's pantry. I'm not sure how much noise you'll make going through, so go slow. Do you have a weapon?"

"No."

She sighed and propped her foot on a nearby rock. "Here." He watched, amazed as she drew a knife out of her boot.

"Who are you?" he couldn't help asking, taking the knife.

She shook her head and glanced over her shoulder.

"Later, Keaton Benedict." She tilted her head toward the knife. "Do you know how to use that without killing yourself in the process?"

The knife's wooden handle felt smooth with wear. More than likely it fit the owner like a glove. "Yes, but are you sure?"

"Take it," she said, looking over her shoulder again. "I have more."

Another time and another place, he would have questioned her more, but he had to get inside. He had to get Tilly away from Elise. He gripped the knife tightly. Whatever the cost.

"Thank you…." he said, wanting at least her name.

She hesitated only a moment before replying, "Kaja."

"Thank you, Kaja," he said and opened the heavy door that would lead him to Tilly.

CHAPTER 25

Tilly would have laughed with glee if Elise didn't look so wild and unhinged. The gun had misfired. Elise had been completely prepared to shoot Maggie, but the gun misfired.

It took her brain a second to absorb the reality of what that meant. Elise was unarmed. For the moment, at least, until she could get her gun working again.Tilly scrambled to her feet, but twisted her ankle in the process and fell back down.

Damn it.

Her heart pounded and fear made it difficult to breath, but damn it, if she couldn't stand, she'd crawl. Sobbing, she slowly made her way toward the butler's pantry. She'd moved only a few feet before the metallic click of a gun left her frozen. Elise stood directly in her path.

"Good girl," Elise said. "Now, stand up, and get back over here."

Tilly slowly got to her feet, wincing when she put any weight on her hurt ankle. Elise held the gun. Maybe it wouldn't work. She'd stay right where she was.

Elise narrowed her eyes and pulled the trigger. The wooden floor just to Tilly's left exploded.

"I just wanted to assure you that the gun is working. If I wanted to hurt you, you'd be dead." She motioned Tilly forward with the gun.

Tilly must have hesitated a bit too long because Elise walked up to her and pressed the gun against her forehead. "I'm not going to tell you again, get over there and sign the paper now."

Elise's hand trembled, her finger looking dangerously close to pulling the trigger.

Tilly couldn't think of what else to do; she didn't even have a way to leave Keaton a note. The finality of her situation overcame her, and tears gathered in her eyes. This was not the way she planned to go out. Not like this. Not at the hands of a crazy woman.

She held her hands up and took a step backward toward the table.

"Hell, I'm tired of this," Elise said. "I'll forge your name. Say goodbye."

From behind Elise came a soft click. It was faint, but loud enough that Elise frowned and the gun dropped the slightest bit. Tilly couldn't hold back her gasp as Keaton flew up behind Elise and held her with one arm around her chest.

"I have a knife," he whispered, all the while looking at Tilly. "Drop the gun, and I won't kill you."

Get away. Get away, Tilly's mind chanted and she took a step to the side.

"If you're smart, you won't move again," Elise said, obviously thinking he wasn't serious, but from the way she jumped and the way the last of the sentence was spoken in a high squeak, he obviously showed her otherwise.

"I don't want to kill you, but I swear to god, if you don't drop the gun now, I will." The icy chill of his voice and the determination in his eyes told Tilly he spoke true.

Sobbing, Elise tried to push away from Keaton, but his hold on her was too strong. Unfortunately, he couldn't grab the gun without either letting go of her or the knife.

The gun rose again, and Keaton barely had time to yell, "Drop, Tilly!" before the shot was fired.

"TILLY! TILLY!" Someone called. From her place on the ground, she couldn't tell who it was. There was so much blood. Blood everywhere. All over her. All over the floor.

Her ears rang, but she didn't hurt. Shouldn't she hurt somewhere with all the blood everywhere?

Multiple hands gently pushed her to her back and she looked up and found Keaton watching her.

"Are you okay?" he asked.

She glanced to his shirt. He was covered in blood, too. She reached out a hand to touch him. Had he been shot? Was all the blood his?

He took her hand. "I think she's just in shock," he said to someone she couldn't see. "I don't think she was hit."

But if he wasn't hit and she wasn't hit, that meant...

"Elise?" she whispered.

Something a lot like pain, but closer to pity crossed his face. "She's gone, Tilly. She shot herself."

Tilly struggled to sit up and see for herself, but the hands pushed her back down.

"In a minute," Keaton said. "Let's make sure you're not injured first."

Knowing it was for the best, she let the paramedics

poke and prod her until everyone was assured she was only suffering from shock.

"Maggie?" she asked Keaton between sips of the water someone had handed her.

The house that had been so eerily quiet before was now teeming with activity. There were medics and police everywhere. Not too far away and at her right side, someone was covered by a white sheet. She assumed it was Elise's body, but she didn't ask. There wasn't anything else covered in a sheet and she hoped that meant Maggie was on her way to the hospital.

Keaton sat behind her, practically holding her in his lap. He leaned forward. His very presence calmed her. "Last I heard, she was being taken into surgery. It's touch and go, but they're hopeful."

He wasn't able to say more because Alyssa came up to them. "Ms. Brock, I'm going to need to take your statement." She looked at her notes and frowned. "Mr. Benedict, you mentioned there was someone at the window when you made it here?"

Knox walked up behind the police officer. "I saw her, too."

"But neither one of you got any information?" Alyssa asked.

"She told me her name was Kaja, but it was very strange she knew about the hidden passageway in the house. I've never seen it." He lifted his head to talk to Knox. "Did you know our house had a secret passageway?"

"No, and that's a damn shame because I'd have loved to have played in there as a kid."

"I bet Kipling didn't know, either. There's no way he could have kept that information to himself." Keaton knew his older brother. Had the secret passageway been common knowledge, they would have tormented their parents and house guests over the years.

"Unfortunately, I can't do anything with only a first name. No matter how unusual it is."

Keaton described her to Alyssa as best he could, but honestly, he told her, at the time he was more concerned about getting to Tilly and getting her away from Elise. He didn't take notice of more than the fact she was female.

"And she carried a knife in an ankle holster?" Alyssa added with a raised eyebrow.

"That, too."

Alyssa finished up with a few more questions, told Tilly she'd be back later to interview her, and left. Kipling had made it to the house by that time, muttering under his breath about the damn traffic and how the police almost wouldn't let him in his own house.

He gave Tilly a hug and looked with sadness at the white sheet covering Elise. "I should be the one to tell the Germains. They shouldn't have to hear about it from the cops."

Tilly imagined how upset the Germains would be. Elise had been their only child. It didn't matter Elise had tried to kill her, no parent should outlive their child.

The coroner arrived to move the body. Keaton tried to shield her, but she saw it just the same. Without warning, she started to cry, even as Keaton tightened his hold on her.

"I'm taking her upstairs," Keaton said to someone, and the next thing she knew, she was being lifted into his arms. She clung to him as he carried her up to his bedroom and placed her on his bed. He joined her, holding her close as she cried.

She cried for Elise's parents, the child Elise had been, the loss of her friendship, and for the Elise who might have been. She cried because she was scared, because she almost died, and though she didn't understand why, because she felt guilty for being okay when Maggie was fighting for her life, and Elise was dead.

She clung to Keaton as if he was her sustainer and savior, and when she'd finished crying, she smiled because he was both. She snuggled into his arms and with a voice hoarse from crying, she told him she loved him.

His voice shook when he answered. "I love you, too. And I've never been more scared in my life than today when I thought I was going to lose you."

She turned to him. "I was scared I'd never see you again."

He kissed her forehead. "I think if I could hold you like this for the rest of my life, I'd be a happy man."

"I'm never letting you go, Keaton Benedict."

"I wouldn't go anywhere if you did, Tilly Brock."

CHAPTER 26

Two Months Later

"Keaton!" Tilly wasn't sure what Keaton was thinking about disappearing hours before the big outside party to announce the new addition to Benedict Industries. Especially since the new division had been completely his doing.

Kipling told her he thought he saw Keaton headed around the back of the house near the flower garden.

"And when you see him," he added, seconds before Tilly went outside to look. "Tell him to get his worthless ass to me ASAP."

His huge smile didn't fit with his words and she stood there for a few seconds until Kipling said, "Tilly. Flower garden. Now."

"Right," she said and headed outside. It was miserably hot, and the humidity hit her as soon as she stepped outside. It felt as if she'd been wrapped in a steaming towel. Kipling had ordered tents for the party, but those had been setup on the other side of the garden. She hoped they had some sort of fans in them.

She rounded the corner of the house, ready to call his name again when she saw him. He was turned away from her, but stood in a way that allowed her to admire his profile. His hands were in the pockets of his navy suit, and he stared at something out of her line of sight.

She took a step and a twig snapped under her foot. Keaton spun around at the sound and smiled when he saw her.

"What are you doing?" she asked walking to him. "Guests will be arriving any minute, Maggie is not resting like I told her, the caterer is mumbling something about missing shrimp, and Kipling said he wants your ass ASAP."

He looked completely oblivious to everything she'd just said. "Come here," he said, pulling her close to his chest.

"Did you hear anything I just said?"

"Yes."

"Are you going to go back into the house?"

"Not yet."

"Not yet? But the party's starting, and Maggie..." her voice trailed off. He was smiling and nodding at everything she said. "You're not listening at all."

"I am, but it can all wait."

She opened her mouth to speak, but couldn't think of anything to say in response, so she closed it.

Keaton, on the other hand, had no problem finding words. "Almost losing you showed me that none of us are guaranteed anything other than the here and now. And the best part of my here and now is you. But I'm a selfish SOB and I want more. I want you to be the best part of my years to come. I love you, Tilly Brock." He let go of her to reach in his pocket again and shifted to kneel on one knee.

Tilly's hand flew to her mouth, because surely he

wasn't, but tears prickled her eyes, because *oh-my-god,* he was.

"Will you marry me?" he asked, holding out a diamond solitaire.

The tears were no longer prickling. They were running down her cheeks and it felt silly because she'd never been happier than she felt at that moment. One word kept repeating in her head and she finally got her lips to move and say it.

"Yes."

THE CROWD GATHERED on grounds of Benedict House hushed at the sound of silver tapping glass.

"Excuse me. May I have your attention?"

Keaton smiled and turned to his older brother.

"Thank you all for coming to help us celebrate this historic day for Benedict Industries," Kipling said. "As most of you are aware, helping others has always been a passion for my baby brother, Keaton. For him, it's not enough to give to those in need, he wants to teach them to be leaders, so they can in turn reach others. And that's what his new division of Benedict Industries, the Benedict Community Development Division will do. Of course, he can't do it alone and he's smart enough to know a good thing when he sees it, which is why at his side will be Tilly Brock."

Keaton put his arm around Tilly and gave her a quick kiss on the cheek.

"We've known Tilly for years and are thrilled to officially welcome her to Benedict Industries. And though she has always been family, I hope Keaton doesn't mind if I let slip that soon she will become an official member of the

Benedict family. Hold that hand up and show everyone your ring, Tilly."

"No, he didn't," Tilly moaned.

"So much for keeping it quiet for now." Keaton shook his head, but took Tilly's left hand and lifted it above their heads. A few of the men near him, slapped his back and whispered congratulations. Everyone else clapped.

When the crowd quieted down, Kipling continued. "This has been a difficult summer for the Benedicts, and we truly appreciate you standing by us. I for one, could not be happier that my little brother has found a lifetime companion in Tilly and I look forward to the day when she becomes my little sister." He raised his glass. "So would you all raise your glass and join me in toasting my brother, Keaton Benedict and his fiancé, Tilly Brock, soon to be Benedict."

After that, it was a long while before the congratulations ceased. Tilly joked that she was smiling so much, her cheeks hurt. But she looked happy and that made Keaton content.

While Keaton knew she really didn't mind Kipling spilling the beans, he saw her flinch at the words, "little sister." Elise had never given him her evidence nor told him where it was. As a result, he'd decided not to tell his brothers about the sister who'd died before they knew she existed. Tilly didn't like keeping secrets, but agreed there was no need for them to know. At least not now. Not while everything was so raw and exposed.

"Sorry about that," Kipling said, coming up beside him and giving him a one armed hug.

"No you're not," Tilly teased. "Don't even pretend to be remorseful."

Kipling laughed, and Keaton realized it'd been far too long since he heard his older brother do so.

"Why, Mr. Benedict, I'm impressed. You might actually have a heart in that chest of yours."

The three of them turned at the sound of Alyssa's voice. Keaton was shocked that Kipling kept his smile intact.

"Officer Adams," he said in reply. "Have you been eyeing my chest? I'd be happy to take my shirt off so you can get a better look, but I'll warn you, I expect you to do the same in return."

Alyssa ignored him and turned to Keaton. "Congratulations on your engagement."

"Thank you." Keaton kicked his brother. "What can we help you with, Officer?"

"I apologize for stopping by unannounced, but we have an update on the twins, and I thought you would like to know."

"Did you find the man in the picture?" Tilly asked.

"We have." She winced. "Rather, we found part of his remains. He appears to have drowned."

"He appears?" Kipling asked, crossing his arms across his chest. "You don't think he did?"

"I think it's a bit too tidy, but unfortunately, the local wildlife got to him before we did. However, he also left a note confessing to Raven, Mandy and Mindy's murders, as well as the informant from the shelter."

Keaton glanced at Tilly, but she just nodded. She'd told him not too long ago that she assumed the wannabe photographer had been killed.

"He did tell us where to find her body, so we have a dive crew looking," Alyssa said. "I guess if we find her that might be the evidence we need to put the cases to rest."

"And yet, you still don't think it was him?" Kipling asked again.

"I'm not sure, but I'll find out." Alyssa grinned at him. "You're not the only one who's thorough, Mr. Benedict."

"I'd say I look forward to seeing you in action, but the truth is, I'm rather glad you don't have any lingering reasons to stop by. No offense intended." He held out his hand.

Alyssa shook it. "None taken. Goodbye, Mr. Benedict."

Kipling nodded and watched her leave. Keaton was shocked when he turned back immediately without ogling her ass.

"Well," Kipling said. "There's that."

Keaton didn't think he imagined the melancholy expression Kipling had for a brief moment. He was getting ready to ask him about it when Maggie called his name and waved him to come to her.

She'd had a precarious and lengthy recovery, mostly due to her age. The brothers had offered her a hefty retirement package, but she'd scoffed and said she'd rather be dead than to not work for her boys anymore.

Keaton told Tilly he'd be right back and jogged over to see what Maggie needed.

"I'm looking for Mr. Knox," she said. "But I don't see him out here."

"He went back inside after the toast. Is something wrong?" Keaton asked.

"Mmm," Maggie said. "I think I need Mr. Knox."

"Why?"

Maggie pointed to the approaching figure he hadn't seen before. "Ms. Bea."

"I'll handle this," he said, giving her a pat on the back. "Will you go tell Tilly I'll be a few more minutes?" He waited for Bea to make it to him. "Knox isn't free at the moment. Is there something I can help you with?"

He didn't mean to sound confrontational, but he was afraid he did.

He could see why his brother was captivated by the tall and willowy attorney. She was pale, with a few barely there freckles across her nose, red hair, and piercing blue eyes. He wouldn't be surprised if it turned out Knox had made a pass at her.

She bit her bottom lip and glanced nervously around the lawn at the numerous guests. "I forgot this was today."

So Knox *had* invited her. Interesting.

"Bea?" Knox asked, appearing from the side of the house.

Bea looked relieved Knox had shown up, but regardless, Keaton wasn't leaving them alone. No way. Not when this woman had the ability to rip his brother apart emotionally.

"Knox," she said, looking sideways at Keaton. He stood his ground and crossed his arm. It wasn't until he raised an eyebrow that she continued. "I'm sorry to just show up like this." She took a deep breath. "Oh, god. This is harder than I thought. I should go."

"Bea. Stop." Knox sounded more pained than he had in weeks. "What's wrong."

Belatedly, Keaton realized Alyssa hadn't said anything about the note that guy left taking responsibility for the attack on Bea.

Who had that been?

She took a deep breath and wiped her damp cheeks. "I had roses delivered to me today. I thought they were from you, but they..." She blinked the tears out of her eyes. "The note said, *Just a little RSVP to let you know I'll be back to finish what I started.*"

EPILOGUE

Though originally I'd been excited to get on a bus and go wherever the soonest departure happened to be going, now I was just tired. Even still, I stood back, taking my time to observe the bus station. At first, I thought everything was clear, but just when I lifted my foot to step out of my hiding place, one of King's henchmen appeared from out of the men's room.

Damn it. How did they catch up so quickly?

But, of course, I knew. King had trained me, of course, he'd figure out my plan to get out of town. By now, he was sure to have men scattered all over the city and especially at bus stations.

Fuck it all. Why had I gone to the Benedicts?

Because I was an idiot.

However, the important thing was not to become a dead idiot. Doing that meant staying one step ahead of King. It wouldn't be easy, and it was damn near impossible on my own. I needed help.

I knew exactly who to turn to for help. It was a brilliant idea. Perfect. The last person anyone would think I'd approach.

I turned around, ready to put my new plan in motion, but

instead ran straight into King's enforcer. He caught me completely off guard, and within seconds, had his hand around my mouth and his other arm holding me tightly to him.

I struggled, but it was no use. He was much too strong.

His deep chuckle sent shockwaves of fear through my body. "All he ever talked about was Jade this and Jade that. Made you out to be some sort of super hero and yet, look at how easily I took you down. It's downright pathetic."

I couldn't allow myself to care about his insults. My focus had to be on one thing and one thing only: getting away. Turning a deaf ear to him, I lifted a knee with the hope he'd think I was aiming at his groin.

He pushed my knee away as if swatting a bothersome fly. "You really think I'm stupid enough to let you do that?"

"No." I reached for the knife I'd replaced in my boot after giving Keaton the other one. Moving quickly, I jerked it out and aimed at his neck. "But you're stupid enough to let me do this."

I'd underestimated him, though, and he turned at the last second, which meant I didn't kill him. However, the gash I left in his shoulder hurt enough that his arms loosened.

As soon as I felt his arms slacken a tiny bit, I was off. I didn't stop until I was far enough away to be safe. I stood, bent over with my hands on my knees gasping for breath with one thought running through my mind.

Charleston was no longer an option.

AUTHOR'S NOTE

Dear Reader,

Charleston has always been my favorite southern city, though it wasn't until I graduated from college that I visited for the first time. I went with college friends, and like most recent grads, we were high on life and low on funds. Needless to say, a great time was had by all. It only made sense to set a suspense series there.

It's a bit intimidating to step out of your writing box. I've always been a die hard pantster, but since suspense was a new genre for me, I sat down and attempted the nightmare known as PLOTTING.

You're going to have to take my word that I really truly tried to follow the plot I wrote. But my brain has never worked that way and halfway through PERILOUS KISS, I wrote a scene with a young woman who refused to listen to me when I told her she didn't have a place outside of the homeless shelter.

Jade, being Jade, proceeded to not only show up outside the shelter, but also rearranged first PERILOUS KISS and then most of the other two novels. I told her she was a troublemaker and was screwing up THE ENTIRE SERIES. She only nodded and said, "Good, it needed to be screwed up."

She turned out to be right. Those pesky characters always are.

Till next time,

Tara

SEDUCTIVE LIES

**DON'T MISS KNOX AND BEA IN
SEDUCTIVE LIES**

Bea Jacobs didn't think she'd find anything when Knox
Benedict asked for her opinion on old business files. But
after being warned to stay away from the Benedicts and
nearly beaten to death by an unknown assailant, she's
certain there's something there. Though she's willing to
keep digging, her first priority is keeping Knox safe.

Knox is concerned with two things: finding out who hurt Bea and winning her back. He'll do anything for her, except leave her alone. He knows she loves him, but suspects she's keeping something secret.

Bea isn't the only one. Secrets are everywhere, from long lost letters to their own family members to the reappearance of a troubled young woman with her own burdens. Bea and Knox have the most unexpected secret, but someone close is hiding a deadly one, and they're going to show Bea what happens when she ignores warnings.

Chapter One

Bea had to get out of the conference room before the man across the table tried to kill her.

Logically, she told herself he wasn't dangerous. Even though she knew better than to judge people based upon their appearance, the man in question was short, on the stocky side, and she could probably take him, thanks to the self defense course she'd completed last week. Assuming of course he didn't pull a gun on her. No, what tested her sanity was the pen he kept tapping on the table. The *tap, tap, tap* didn't stop and she couldn't get out of her head because it brought back thoughts of the man who almost *had* killed her.

Tap. Tap. Tap.

Sweat trickled down her spine.

Tap. Tap. Tap.

Her stomach felt sour.

Tap. Tap. Tap.

She closed her eyes, took deep breaths, and tried everything she knew to make it stop. Nothing worked. Not counting backwards. Not running through multiplication tables. Not even picturing herself relaxing on a deserted beach. Damn it, she was going to have a full-blown panic attack sitting in the middle of her senior partner's meeting with a client he wanted her to co-represent.

Tap. Tap. Tap.

She took another deep breath. This was not happening. She wasn't going to let it. But her heart began to race and she knew she was fighting a losing battle.

"Ms. Jacobs?" Skip, the senior partner, asked. "Your thoughts?"

Shit. "I, um, agree with your analysis."

The pen stopped tapping and she was able to suck in another breath. Deep even breaths. Surely the meeting wouldn't go on much longer and she'd be able to get up and walk. Splash some water on her face and maybe go outside for some fresh air.

Skip raised an eyebrow. "Really? You were most forceful in your opposition yesterday."

The pen started tapping once again.

Tap. Tap. Tap.

Tap. Tap. Tap.

She was going to be sick. She pushed back from her chair and stood on wobbly legs. "If you'll excuse me."

Without waiting for a reply, she darted from the room as quickly as possible, managing not to crash into Vicky, the office admin, who was bringing coffee into the conference room.

"Ms. Jacobs?" Vicky called as she raced by.

Bea didn't slow down or turn around. She made it to the bathroom and shut the door, sagging against it, and forcing herself to take deep breaths. For a brief second, she thought she was going to be fine, but the panic she'd tried to hold back clawed its way up her throat. Her stomach lurched in response and she stumbled forward, desperate to make it to a toilet before losing her breakfast.

After, she rinsed her mouth out and leaned her head against the cool tile on the wall. She was still breathing heavy and she balled her fists in defiance, even as her mind replayed the seconds leading up to her attack: the sudden shift in the air alerting her something was wrong and the feel of rough hands pushing her against a brick wall. In what she thought was a cruel mind trick, all of her senses had been super-heightened and now, almost six weeks later, she could still feel him breathing on her, still smell the stench of human waste in the alley he dragged her into, and through it all, still hear the *tick tick tick* of his watch.

She stood up with new determination. The assholes who hurt her weren't going to win. She'd be damned if they were going to get the best of her.

She would force herself to listen to pen tapping for hours on end if that's what it took. Maybe she should get some professional help like they'd recommended at the hospital after her attack. At the time, she'd thought she'd be fine if she could only get home and she'd thrown away the business cards they'd given her.

Little did she know that getting home was only one step in the seemingly three thousand needed for recovery. And in no way had it ever crossed her mind she'd still be having panic attacks weeks later. Knox would be upset if he knew.

Knox . . .

He was an entirely different problem. Her gaze dropped to her bare left hand and she had to squeeze her eyes closed so the tears that always seemed to follow thoughts of him didn't fall. But trying not to think of his devilishly handsome grin, his tousled dirty blond hair, and his utterly devastating charm, only made her think of them more.

Someone knocked on the door.

"Ms. Bea."

It was Vicky, bless her heart.

"Just a minute." Bea splashed water on her face and wiped her eyes. A quick glance in the mirror told her she looked like shit, but there was little she could do to fix it at this point.

"You okay?" Vicky asked when Bea finally opened the door.

"Getting that way."

Vicky pressed her lips together. Probably because she

knew a lie when she heard one. Bea wasn't getting better. Some days she felt as if she were barely functioning. It didn't help that Vicky was a mother hen and had sharp eyes.

"I don't feel so good," Bea said. "I'm going to work from home. I'll call Skip when I get there."

Vicky nodded. "I'm going to let you go, but I don't like you being alone so much."

Once she made it home and she called and left a voice mail for Skip, she pulled on her pajamas and curled up on her couch with her comfy blanket. It was absurd to even have a blanket out this time of the year, much less to use one. But for some reason, it made her feel safe to have it wrapped around her. Silly, of course, the blanket being a thin piece of fabric.

It was probably because *he* gave it to her. She snorted at the way her brain worked. Of course it was because he gave it to her. For what other reason would she bring the soft material to her nose in order to see if some small trace of his scent still lingered there?

But the softest of fabric was nothing even close to him and she shrugged the blanket from her shoulders. She turned her laptop on so she wouldn't think about him anymore, only to have the project she'd been working on with him before the accident pop up. She shook her head, hating she now kept track of time and events that way.

The Johnson case? Oh, yes, that was *before.*

The Turner case, however, that was *after.*

Another thing she needed to take care of and fix. Thinking in those terms gave her attackers too much power over her, her life, and her future. That type of thinking stopped today. Right this minute.

She thought about opening the file containing the

project, but with the memory of her recent panic attack fresh in her mind, she didn't dare. Too afraid thinking about anything having to do with the Benedicts would stir up a pot of trouble she wasn't prepared to deal with.

Since the project was a personal matter, from Knox, it shouldn't bother her to leave the file unopened. But it did. Knox asked her privately to look into some old issues from his family's shipping company, Benedict Industries. His older brother, Kipling, had thought the human resources records looked off. She'd agreed, and started looking into the personnel files he gave her. For hours, she searched for any red flag, no matter how small, not knowing that doing so would lead to her attack.

That last bit had come to her days later in the hospital. When she remembered the man with the ticking watch telling her to stay away from Knox. Or else. She recalled the cold sweat covering her body the moment she remembered and the way goose bumps rippled her skin. But most of all, she remembered the despair she felt, knowing she had to end her relationship with Knox. Because the next time she met the ticking man, he wouldn't leave her alive. And Knox would be his next target.

Her phone rang and she grabbed it without looking, thinking it was Skip. "Hello."

"Ms. Jacobs, this is Mandy at Dean Family Law. Your divorce papers are here and ready to be signed."

EXPOSED DESIRE

Want more?
Don't miss the explosive last book,
EXPOSED DESIRE...

*Kipling and Alyssa join together to fight for the future one man
is determined they won't live to see...*

ABOUT THE AUTHOR

Even though she graduated with a degree in science, Tara knew she'd never be happy doing anything other than writing. Specifically, writing love stories.

She started with a racy BDSM story and found she was not quite prepared for the unforeseen impact it would have. Nonetheless, she continued and The Submissive Series novels would go on to be both *New York Times* and *USA Today* bestsellers. One of those, THE MASTER, was a 2017 RITA finalist for Best Erotic Romance. Over one million copies of her books have been sold worldwide.

www.tarasueme.com

Also by Tara Sue Me

THE SUBMISSIVE SERIES:

The Submissive

The Dominant

The Training

The Chalet*

Seduced by Fire

The Enticement

The Collar

The Exhibitionist

The Master

The Exposure

The Claiming*

The Flirtation

Mentor's Match

The Mentor & The Master*

Top Trouble

Nathaniel's Gift*

The Pretender*

The Anniversary*

RACK ACADEMY SERIES:

Master Professor

Headmaster

Master of Pleasure

BACHELOR INTERNATIONAL:

Mister Temptation (Previously published as AMERICAN ASSHOLE)

Mister Irresistible

Mister Impossible

THE DATE DUO:

The Date Dare

The Date Deal

WALL STREET ROYALS:

FOK

Big Swinging D

All or None

THE BENEDICT BROTHERS

(Edited/rewritten version of Sons of Broad)

Perilous Kiss

Seductive Lies

Exposed Desire

OTHERS:

Madame President

Bucked

Her Last Hello

Altered Allies (currently unavailable)

*eNovella